Tales of Harriford Grange

Volume 1

Elizabeth J. Smith

This is a work of fiction. Names, characters, businesses, places, events, locales, and incidents are either the products of the author's imagination or used in a fictitious manner. Any resemblance to actual persons, living or dead, or actual events is purely coincidental.

All rights reserved. This book or any portion thereof may not be reproduced or used in any manner whatsoever without the express written permission of the author except for the use of brief quotations in a book review.

Contact via https://authorelizabethjsmith.com/contact/

© 2020 by Elizabeth J. Smith

ISBN: 9798671194371

Author: Elizabeth J. Smith
Cover Design: Marble Fox Designs

Foreword.....7

Acknowledgements.....9

The Doctor's Daughter.....11

The Farrier's Girl.....37

The Butcher's Lady.....55

The Shopkeeper's Love.....79

Foreword

Dear Reader,

    I had such fun spending long hours with the characters of Harriford Grange. Harriford Grange is a fictional small town set in the south of England. I purposely left the exact time ambiguously situated between the mid 1800s and the early 1900s, and I used a mixture of past and modern vernacular to paint a picture from my own writer's voice. My characters are not without their flaws, but I hope I left each better than I found them. They are very dear to me, and I hope you will love them as much as I do.

    The Doctor's Daughter is a comedy of errors as the new doctor seeks to woo his nurse, the former doctor's daughter. Can he overcome her false perceptions and win her heart?

    Prejudice can take many forms as is seen in *The Farrier's Girl*. What will it take to break the ice between the new farrier and the wealthiest girl in town?

    In *The Butcher's Lady*, learning to trust takes center stage. When the butcher discovers the woman he loves is being exploited, can he earn her trust and kindle her love?

    The last story is a tale of second chances and forgiveness. Will an ex-convict be able to overcome his past to be *The Shopkeeper's Love*?

    Thank you for taking the time to read my stories. I'll leave you with the sentiment, if not the words, of Miss Jane Austen: All of my characters shall have happy endings.

In Him,
Elizabeth J. Smith

Acknowledgements

Thank you to my husband Jonathan and my friend Leah for your help and encouragement in bringing these stories to print. Only chocolate and baked goods can express the depth of my appreciation for your friendship.

The Doctor's Daughter

Exquisite. It was the only word to describe her. Dr. Colm Byrne followed the vision of loveliness from the small stone chapel and paused to observe her as she spoke with Mrs. Stevens, the preacher's wife. Striding forward, he tipped his hat toward the two ladies, hopes high for an introduction. Mrs. Stevens gave him a knowing look before turning to her companion.

"My dear Edith, I don't believe you've met Dr. Byrne. Doctor, this is Miss Edith Caldwell, the daughter of..."

"The late Dr. Caldwell," Colm finished. "I'm so sorry for your loss, madam."

The lady's dark eyebrows rose in alarm as she regarded him. "I thank you, sir. I wasn't expecting your arrival until Friday at the earliest. I'm afraid we haven't completed our move to the guest cottage just yet."

"No matter," he replied, enjoying the picture her soft chestnut curls made with her slightly tanned skin. "I made arrangements at the inn until Saturday."

Watching with obvious interest, Mrs. Stevens inquired whether he had plans for luncheon. He did not. She heartily extended an invitation stating that he and Edith would nicely round out their foursome. He took his eyes off the beautiful Edith Caldwell long enough to thank her and happily accept. After the good lady excused herself, he extended his arm to Miss Caldwell, offering to walk her over to the parsonage.

Edith accepted his arm, and they strolled slowly toward the cozy stone structure. Upon entering the front garden, the gentleman at her side began to admire the colorful flowers. He quizzed her knowledge of the subject until reaching a large bush of blue-pink clusters. He leaned closer to the bush, bringing his face level with hers. Then, he turned his admiring gaze on her.

"Hydrangea, Dr. Byrne. One of my favorites."

"Beautiful."

Her face heated slightly as she noticed the gold flecks in his dark brown eyes and his slightly crooked, frecklecovered nose. One side of his mouth tipped up as he resumed his full height. Suddenly realizing she was still clutching his arm, she dropped her hand to her side and turned toward Mr. and Mrs. Stevens as they entered the garden.

Once inside, Edith helped Mrs. Stevens finish her luncheon preparations, and they all sat down at the table. After praying for the food, they passed around the roast, carrots, potatoes, and freshly-baked yeast rolls. Edith watched the gentleman across from her as secretly as possible. He cut a fine figure, taller than her and not overly muscular. Something about his wavy light brownish-red hair and freckles gave him a boyish look, while his dark eyes and firm jaw showed a pleasing maturity. Yes, he would do nicely. The patients would adore him.

He caught her watching him but couldn't decipher her conclusion. She smiled freely and equally at each diner and held eye contact with him on more than one occasion. Her complexion was youthful and rosy, but her manners and bearing spoke of someone older than his eight-and-twenty years.

After custard and tea, Edith excused herself, saying she had work to do at home. Colm made to leave as well, and once outside, he offered to walk her home. She took his arm once again, and he noticed how well her hand fit into the crook of his arm. They strolled down the street and stopped before a large white clapboard house fronted with an even more impressive garden. A white sign read *Harriford Grange Clinic*. She pointed to the small stone house next door.

"That's the guest cottage, Dr. Byrne. My maid Tilly and I will be moving in there so that you may live in the doctor's quarters in the main house."

"I hate to uproot you from your home, Miss Caldwell. I'll happily move into the guest cottage."

"That's very kind of you, Doctor, but we are quite satisfied with this arrangement. Plus, you may need access to the office during the night, and it would be..."

"No need to explain. I will do whatever you wish. I came here to serve." He patted her lace gloved hand, wishing she'd left the gloves off. He stopped her as she started to pull her hand away.

"Will you be attending the evening service?"

"Indeed, sir. I wouldn't think of missing."

He swallowed before taking the leap. "Would you mind if I escorted you this evening? I can be here in plenty of time." He almost added something about an office tour before biting his tongue and reminding himself she was busy.

She regarded him for a moment before nodding. "If you wish."

His heart soared as he walked back to the inn. He may have just arrived in Harriford Grange, but Miss Edith Caldwell had already claimed his heart.

Edith smiled to herself as she closed the polished oak front door. Dr. Colm Byrne was delightful, and she was eager to work with him. She warmed at the remembrance of his gaze and invitation. Handsome, indeed he was. This reverie lasted until she glanced in the looking glass in the foyer. Brown hair showing a few silver threads and imperfect, pocked skin brought her back to reality. While her curly brown hair was often denoted as her best feature, small pox as a child, along with a slight problem with acne, had rendered her skin less than smooth and often a little blotchy. At thirty-five, she was still considered "pretty," but anything more than that had rarely been ascribed to her. Her heart panged at a long pushed aside remembrance, but she shoved it back into its corner. She ran upstairs to change. She had work to do.

Colm arrived forty-five minutes before the service and pulled the doorbell. He was surprised when Miss Caldwell, not the maid, answered the door.

"Hello! I'm not quite ready. Usually Tilly answers the door, but today is one of her days off." The last part trailed after her as she hurried down a long hallway.

Not wanting to be left behind, Colm followed her to a small enclosed porch at the rear of the building. Edith turned abruptly and covered her heart. "I didn't realize you'd followed me. I needed to fetch my boots, and..." she glanced frantically about before spotting her query, "my hat. I'll be ready in just a moment. You're quite early, you know."

"No hurry," he said, following her back to the front of the house. She frowned before the glass as she pinned on her hat. He saw nothing which should have caused this reaction but decided not to state that thought aloud.

"Would you like a tour, then? Is that why you're early?"

He forced his thoughts to concentrate on her words. "A tour? Yes. Why not?"

Nodding curtly, she motioned to a closed door to the left of the massive front door. They entered a dimly lit waiting room filled with mismatched chairs and a few small tables. Large windows covered in gauzy curtains let in the late afternoon light. A neat mahogany desk was stationed before the door to the examination room. He noted with satisfaction the space's cleanliness before following her through the door. He was surprised to find not one, but two exam rooms, as well as a well-equipped washing station, a lavatory, and a large doctor's office. Closets housed linens, supplies, and an extensive pharmacy.

"As you can see, we have everything a country doctor would need. My father insisted on only the best and most sanitary conditions. Marjorie Robards does the cleaning and front desk work, while Tilly Grant keeps the house and guest cottage. I'm trained as a nurse, and I also do just about every other job other than doctoring." She took a deep breath and waited for his reply.

"You're the nurse," he replied, hiding a grin.

"I am. Is that a problem?"

"No, no. Not at all. I think we'll get along quite well." He smiled what he hoped was an award-winning smile.

She returned his grin. "As do I."

On the walk to church, conversation turned away from work to more neutral subjects. Once again, he marveled at Edith Caldwell, even more eager to beginning his new work.

Once inside the small chapel, Edith caught sight of Louisa Musgrave and caught her breath. The girl had always resembled her brother Roger but now more so than ever. While Roger had been dark, Louisa was fair. Otherwise, they could have been twins – only Louisa's strong jaw was softened with femininity and her broad forehead with curls. She had spent the last year abroad with an aunt and had bloomed and blossomed into a beautiful young woman. And, Edith smirked, Louisa seemed fully aware of that fact.

"Edith, dear Edith! I'm home!" Louisa squealed, pulling her into a hug. Edith returned the hug with equal vigor. She had always been fond of the girl.

"My dear Louisa, you look so well! I can't wait to hear all about your year. I imagine your letters only told half of all the things you experienced."

"Oh, yes! I could write volumes, if only I were given to writing." At this point, Louisa noticed the handsome young doctor standing rather close behind Edith. She arched her brow and leaned close. "And who is this, pray tell?"

"Louisa Musgrave, I have the pleasure of introducing you to Dr. Colm Byrne, my father's replacement."

Louisa had the presence of mind to express her sympathy for Dr. Caldwell's passing before turning her bright smile on the doctor. Edith stole away to her seat as they exchanged pleasantries.

"Is this seat taken?" said Dr. Byrne's now familiar voice, causing her to jump.

"Why, no, Doctor. No one usually sits there."

As Dr. Byrne situated himself next to her, she snuck a glance at Louisa. By her frown, Edith could tell she was not pleased, but the exact reason was unknown. Edith sighed. With Louisa, one knew the truth would come out eventually, whether one wanted to hear it or not.

"So, Doctor, I was raised in the church here."

As with the many Christians he'd met, this remark held an unspoken question. He answered promptly.

"I was raised a Protestant, but my roommate during my undergraduate degree was a member of the church. He invited me to attend services with him, taught me the gospel, and I was baptized soon thereafter. I've been faithfully attending ever since."

This response seemed to greatly please Miss Caldwell, who leaned toward him slightly. "I was twelve. It is such a blessing to be raised in the church, but it's also so easy to take it for granted."

Any further conversation was cut short as a deacon, Edith later pointed out, welcomed the group to the Sunday evening service of the church of Christ at Harriford Grange. He read through a short list of announcements before leading the congregation in an opening prayer. This was followed by *Amazing Grace* sung *a capella*. As he always did, Colm smiled as the voices of brothers and sisters lifted in song to their Lord, unencumbered by mechanical instruments of music. A couple more songs were followed by a Bible reading, and a short devotion led by the elderly and kind Mr. Stevens.

Afterwards, he offered an invitation to those who had not yet put on their Lord in baptism to come be washed in the blood of Jesus in a large baptistery set behind the pulpit. To those already Christian, he prompted them to reflect on their lives in case they needed to repent publically for any sinful actions. Time to partake of the Lord's Supper and giving of the contribution were set aside for those unable to attend the earlier service. Another song and a prayer commenced the meeting. Colm thanked God once again for his good friend who had loved him enough to show him the Way of Truth and for his own willingness to obey it.

He kept an eye on Edith while they both fellowshipped with various brethren. He confirmed at least a dozen times that the doctor would be "in" starting the following Monday. Until then, Dr. Vasser would be on call from nearby Blaketon Commons. He followed her to the vestibule where she appeared to be waiting for him.

"Are you ready to go?" he asked, conscious of her dark green eyes on his face. She nodded assent, and they left the chapel arm in arm. He wished to continue their discussion from before the service, but her yawn stopped him. At the door of the doctor's house, she pulled out her key and bid him good night. On impulse, he took her gloved hand and kissed it.

"Today has been a pleasure, Miss Caldwell," he said with her hand still clasped in his.

"Edith, please," she whispered, trembling slightly. She cleared her throat as if to gain her bearings. "We *will* be working together, Dr. Byrne."

He rubbed his finger over her knuckles before finally releasing her hand. "I'm looking forward to it, Edith." Her name rolled off his tongue like music.

"Good night, Doctor."

"Colm."

"Doctor," she grinned mischievously. "It wouldn't do in front of the patients anyhow for me to call you by your given name."

"See you tomorrow? I thought I might help you and Tilly."

"If you wish. Good night."

He watched her enter her home, which would soon be his, and wandered distractedly back to the inn.

The rest of the week passed like a blur for Edith. Monday and Tuesday, with the handsome doctor's help, were all which were needed to move her and Tilly's belongings to the guest cottage. That done, they spent Wednesday and Thursday moving in the good doctor. More than once, Edith felt a catch in her throat as Dr. Byrne slowly replaced her father's belongings with his own. *Time moves on,* she pondered, *but why must it leave such destruction in its wake?* It was in one of these moments that Dr. Byrne declared that come Friday afternoon, he would declare a holiday, which must of course come with a picnic.

Friday morning started out gloomy, but by afternoon, the sun was shining bright. Tilly had begged off to visit her mother, leaving Edith and Dr. Byrne to picnic on their own. He hefted the picnic basket, and they set off toward the creek. Upon finding a shady spot, Edith spread out a blanket and began removing their picnic fare. Dr. Byrne offered a prayer for the food, and they began to eat in earnest.

Colm lay back on the blanket and looked up at the tree canopy above him. Soft light fell through the glowing leaves and lighted on his pretty companion. He grinned when he caught her watching him, causing her to turn away.

"That was the best picnic fare I've ever had."

"Tilly will be pleased to hear it. She really is a wonderful cook."

He raised himself to a seated position and turned toward Edith. She glanced at him before pretending to be absorbed in some wildlife across the stream.

"Edith, has anyone ever told you you're beautiful?"

"Really, Doctor!" she replied, fanning herself as she turned away. But not before he caught a small grin.

"Indeed, it is true, my fair lady. You must have beaus lined up and down the street!" He said this in a jesting tone, hoping against hope she replied in the negative. However, when she grew pensive, he feared he'd fully blundered.

"I did once. Rather, I had a beau once. He was the only man other than my father who ever called me beautiful."

Colm cleared his throat after her pause grew long. "What happened to him?"

She sighed deeply. "He went off to the war, and well, he didn't come home alive." She stated this matter-of-factly, but he could see the pain in her eyes and hear it in her voice.

"I'm sorry."

"Thank you." Another pause, punctuated with an unseen tear. "He...he wrote me letters, asking me to wait for him, that he would...propose when he returned home."

He turned away to give her a moment to compose herself. "What was his name?"

"Roger. Roger Musgrave. Louisa's older brother."

"I see."

"It was a long time ago. Goodness, almost fifteen years."

"And since then?"

"Harriford Grange isn't exactly brimming with eligible men, Doctor. I threw myself into my nursing studies so I could help my father. I'm happy with my life. God has blessed me despite my loss."

They sat in companionable silence for some time before Colm dared to speak again. Had he erred by bringing to mind her loss? His goal certainly hadn't been to hurt her.

"What might I expect come Monday?" he asked.

"Well, I believe the whole county has been apprised of your arrival, so the office will most likely be busy with everything from stubbed toes to headaches. A few regular patients have their yearly exams, and we'll probably have one or two unexpected emergencies."

"I'd imagine you handle yourself well during emergencies."

"I do my best. It really opens your eyes, this job, but the rewards are worth every trial."

"I agree."

They were a great team, doctor and nurse working perfectly in sync as if it had always been this way. However, as soon as the door was locked behind their last patient each day, his concentration flew out of the window.

He sat in his desk one afternoon watching Edith flit about the hallway, refilling glass jars with cotton swabs and tongue depressors, re-rolling washed bandages, and rearranging the linens. At one point, she pulled out a line of cord and spent a few minutes trying to untangle it. Her brow wrinkled in concentration, and her plump bottom lip was caught between pearly white teeth. After taking in this picture for about two minutes, he jumped up from his chair and held out his hand.

"Allow me."

"Don't bother. I've almost got it." Her eyes didn't move from the knot. He stepped closer and covered her hands with his. At this, she slowly looked up. "Really, I'll have it in a moment."

"I'm sure you will. I just thought I could help."

She relinquished the mass and stepped back as if searching for another task and yet, not wanting to leave. He spent a couple of moments studying the knots before finding the problem. As he coiled the cord around his hand, she thanked him.

"No need. I'm here to serve."

"So you've said...The patients seem to like you. Mrs. Johnson was particularly expressive in her praises."

He laughed, remembering the plump older lady and her shameless flirting. She had called him handsome so many times, he'd lost count.

"She's not my type," he teased, "but I thanked her nonetheless."

"And what is your type, Doctor?" she asked in jest, turning away to put the cord on an upper shelf.

"You."

Her motions stilled, one arm and both feet frozen in a long stretch.

"You flatter me, Doctor," she laughed, although it was somewhat forced. "And flattery will get you anything around here."

What about your heart? He barely stopped himself from blurting out that thought as he stepped up behind her, placing his hand on the small of her back as he put the cord on the shelf. When he turned to look down at her, she wasn't looking at him. In fact, he thought she might be trembling. He pulled his hand away.

"I'm sorry. I…"

She brushed a lose strand of chestnut hair from her face. "No matter. I best finish up my work. I'm sure you would like some peace and quiet to go over your notes. Please excuse me."

He watched her disappear into an exam room before shuffling back to his desk. He'd never been a ladies' man, but he thought he knew how to woo a woman. This one, however, was a bit of a mystery.

In the cool exam room, Edith placed her palm over her rapidly beating heart, wishing it to calm. After a few deep breaths, she looked about the room, seeing but not perceiving her surroundings. He was a flirt. It was as simple as that. After a few more weeks, his attentions would surely turn toward one of the many swooning young ladies who'd graced the office in the past week. That would be best, after all. She was too old for him. Goodness, seven years too old according to what she'd read on his file. Why, he was probably nervous adjusting to a new practice in an unfamiliar town. That was it. He was trying to make sure he was on her good side. The approval of Dr. Caldwell's daughter of the new doctor was very important to the patients of Harriford Grange Clinic. Yes, that was it. She breathed deeply as she forced herself to accept this truth and sweep away the longing she felt for love. They were co-workers and friends. Nothing more. Nothing more.

Sunday morning brought Colm to Edith's front door along with a lovely bouquet of roses, daisies, and dahlias. She answered seconds after his ring, eyes snapping open at the sight of the bountiful bouquet. He gave a slight bow and held it toward her.

"For you, my lady."

She laid the bouquet in her arms and gazed upon it as if it were a newborn babe. "It's lovely. Thank you."

"You're lo...welcome."

She disappeared to put the flowers in a vase, rejoining him a moment later. They walked to the chapel, making small talk about the weather, the flowers, and the upcoming gospel meeting. As he handed her through the door, his eyes lit upon the fair Louisa Musgrave. He determined to have a chat with her as soon as possible.

That time came late Tuesday afternoon when Louisa came in for her yearly check-up. Edith was busy running an errand, making this the ideal moment to question Louisa about her friend.

"Well, Miss Musgrave, you are in perfect health."

"Thank you, Dr. Byrne. That's good to hear."

"Do you mind if I asked you something?"

"Not at all."

Her eyes held curiosity without the hint of flirtation he'd feared. He cleared his throat. "It's about Miss Caldwell."

"Edith?"

"Yes. I find myself in a bit of a predicament."

"You're in love with her."

He ran his fingers through his hair. "Is it that obvious?"

"Indeed, sir. Have you told her?"

"That's the problem. I believe I've courted her from the moment I first laid eyes on her, but my methods don't seem to be working. I'm almost afraid I've frightened her."

"I see."

They were both quiet for a long moment before Louisa breathed a response. "She was practically engaged to my brother Roger when he was killed in the war. She was devastated. I haven't seen her with another man since. Oh, Dr.

Byrne, I would wish more than anything for her to be happily settled! If you truly love her..."

"I do," he whispered, the realization knocking him in the gut.

"Splendid! But, oh, what is you wanted to know?"

"Do you have any idea how I might win her heart?"

Louisa's youthful brow wrinkled in thought. "Flowers?"

"Tried that."

"Dark Chocolates? She loves those."

"I'll put them on the list."

"Um...have you told her how you feel?"

"Practically."

"I'll keep thinking, Doctor. I think this will make a wonderful new project."

"Don't breathe a word of this to Miss Caldwell."

"Of course not, Dr. Byrne! I won't say a thing."

Edith spun away as the exam room door opened to reveal a giggling Louisa followed by a grinning Dr. Byrne. As soon as they caught sight of her, they grew quiet. Louisa scurried away with a breathy "hello" to Edith. The good doctor's face was bright red.

"Hello, *Dr. Byrne*," she said, hating how jealous she felt. He had every right to show attentions to any lady he chose. Had she not recently determined they were not compatible? She was far too old to take his attentions seriously.

"Miss Caldwell. Did you find what I asked for?"

"I did. You sent me on quite a wild goose-chase," *on purpose, no doubt,* "but I'm very good at that sort of thing."

She looked pointedly at him, hoping for...what? A confession?

"Ha, sorry about that...Um, I was thinking about going out for dinner this evening. Would you care to join me, my lady?" he asked, stowing his discomfort and slipping smoothly into chivalry. She barely stopped her jaw from dropping. Had he not just been flirting with Louisa? Maybe she should suggest he ask her instead.

"I'd love to."

"Good," he said, rubbing his hands together.

"I'll have to clean up first."

"I'll come over at six?"

"That should give me enough time."

"Good. Very good."

She watched him practically skip to his office and shut the door behind him. She checked the time and got right to work.

Colm arrived promptly at six with a small box of dark chocolate hearts. He would have bought the largest box they had, but he feared that might be overdoing it. The beauty which opened the door took his breath away. She'd redone her normally tightly knotted chestnut curls into a loose updo, a few escaped ringlets framing her heart-shaped face. Her thick white nurse's dress was replaced with a light green muslin gown which brought out her emerald eyes. He held out the chocolates, unable to form a cohesive thought.

"Dark chocolate hearts. My favorite! How did you know?"

"A little bird told me."

She thanked him and grabbed a light wrap, locking the door behind her. As she took his arm, he noticed she wasn't wearing gloves. He placed his hand casually on hers and relished in the smoothness of her skin. They wandered down the slowly darkening lane toward The Tea Biscuit, the best local eatery. Inside the simply decorated dining room, he led the way to a table in the back corner and pulled out her chair. He seated himself and picked up his menu, glancing frequently over it at his dining companion. After they'd ordered, he leaned forward, not wanting to miss a thing.

"So, Doctor, how are you liking the practice and Harriford Grange?"

"I love...it," he stammered, as if changing his words mid-sentence. He gulped down half of his glass of water.

"I'm glad to hear that. I hope you'll stay for a while. I think you're a perfect fit for our little town."

"Oh, I do plan to stay. Most definitely!"

She laughed at his enthusiasm, even as the seed of jealousy threatened to sprout. She tamped it down and changed the subject.

"Louisa Musgrave is a lovely young woman. I've known her since she was born. I'd say it's about time she was settled happily." Why on earth did she bring that up? She quirked her eyebrow at his reddened face.

"I suppose so."Another gulp and his glass was empty. "Has she any suitors?"

"No one in particular, but I fancy quite a few young men have noticed her since she returned. If one was interested, he better step up now and claim her heart before the others work up the nerve."

"Ah." He looked everywhere but at her before dropping his eyes to his lap. "Say, do you like cricket?"

Stunned for a moment by his sudden change of topic, she shook her head. "I've not had much experience with it, but many of my schoolmates played during recess. Do you?"

"Ever since I was a boy. That's how I," he pointed to his crooked nose, "broke my nose." His equally crooked smile made her grin.

"How did that happen?"

"I was eleven, and one of my mates swung the bat back and hit me square in the face. Not only did I come away with quite a bloody nose, I also discovered my true calling."

"It made you want to become a doctor?"

"Yes, it did," he replied with a laugh. His brown eyes warmed as he held her gaze, sending delightful chills down her arms.

He leaned forward and motioned for her hand. She gave it to him, half hoping he would kiss it. He didn't, but as he held it, he traced circles on its back.

"I told you you were beautiful. I was wrong."

Taken aback, she tried unsuccessfully to pull her hand away. He leaned closer, jostling the table. He dropped her hand as they both scrambled to catch their glasses and tea cups.

"Oh, bother," he exclaimed, tossing his wet napkin. Their food came at that moment, and they ate the rest of their meal in awkward silence.

Wednesday evening's worship service brought Colm a private moment with Louisa. Edith was happily engaged in conversation with a Mrs. Woodburn when he caught Louisa's eye and motioned to the vestibule.

"We've got a problem," he blurted, combing his hair with his shaking fingers. To her inquiring look, he explained. "She thinks I'm in love with you!"

At this, Louisa blanched. He scowled at her, his indignity tempered by relief. He didn't think he was that bad-looking.

"I'm sorry, Dr. Byrne," she replied, once recovered. "I can't imagine what gave her that impression."

"It's alright. So, what do I do about it?"

A sly smile slid across Louisa's pert mouth. "I say we use this to your advantage, Doctor."

"I don't follow."

"Don't you see, if we make her jealous..."

"No, I don't think that's a good idea."

Louisa stomped her foot and crossed her arms. "And why not?"

"Wouldn't it be like lying?"

"Oh, I suppose so. I didn't think of that. So, what do you propose to do?"

"Propose! That's it!"

"You're going to propose to her, even before you know how she feels about you?"

"Yes, and you'll help me!"

She peered dubiously up at him. "And how will I do that?"

"Get her to talk about me. Find out what she thinks, if she would ever love me. While you do that, I'll think about my proposal. It'll have to be the best."

Louisa smiled conspiratorially. "I believe you've come up with a sound plan. I think it just might work!"

"Very good. And thank you, Miss Musgrave, for your help," he replied, bowing gratefully over her hand, at which time, she giggled.

"You're very welcome, Dr. Byrne!"

Edith gawked at the sight. The nerve of him whisking Louisa into the privacy of the vestibule, whispering in her ear, and kissing her hand! How improper! Stomping to the side door, she was out of the chapel and halfway home before she heard fast footsteps behind her.

"Why did you leave without me?" Dr. Byrne asked between gulps of air. She refused to take his arm and hastened onward.

"I think you know very well, Doctor! Louisa is a beautiful young lady, and I consider her my sister, so you best watch yourself! Sneaking off for a private moment, indeed! I've never seen such, such...let go of me!" She jerked away from him, ran inside, and slammed the door in his face.

The chill in the clinic the next morning was palpable. During a brief break, Colm shut himself in his office and slumped into his chair. He never should have confided in Louisa. Edith seemed determined to play matchmaker, albeit a sullen and spiteful one. Could she not see his devotion to her or feel his love? He groaned before slamming his crooked nose into a stack of papers. This was a disaster! At least he still had his proposal to plan. Maybe *that* would get through to her.

Edith greeted Louisa warmly that evening, despite her misgivings about likely topics of conversation.

"What a pleasant surprise, my dear Louisa! Tilly is almost finished with supper. Please join me!"

Louisa looked searchingly about the room. "I was expecting Dr. Byrne to be dining with you."

Edith felt a pang in her heart as she remembered their quarrel.

"He usually does, but he preferred to dine at home this evening. But do join me, my friend! We've not had a chance to catch up!"

Louisa heartily agreed and soon their light soup and sandwich supper was served in the small dining room. While they began with discussion of Louisa's trip abroad, the little minx wiled the conversation back to the handsome Dr. Byrne.

"He is handsome, don't you agree, my dear Edith?"

"Indeed he is, very handsome."

"And his eyes..."

"What about them?"

"Well, what do *you* think about them?"

"They're kind. Have you noticed how the gold flakes perfectly compliment his hair?"

Louisa appeared rather blank at this observation. "I quite like freckles, don't you?"

"I do, and his are rather abundant!" Edith giggled nervously. What was wrong with her? She was fawning over the doctor more than fair Louisa!

Louisa grinned as if she had a secret. "He'd be quite a catch, don't you agree?"

Edith couldn't keep the wistfulness out of her voice as she nodded. "If I were younger, well, never mind."

She cast her gaze down a moment, determined to be happy for her friend, and rose to find Louisa smiling at her.

"What is it?" Edith asked.

"All in due time, sweet sister. All in due time."

Edith rushed to the kitchen to grab their dessert and tea, as well as to soothe her aching heart. If only she were young and pretty, then maybe the handsome doctor would notice her instead.

Louisa lost no time in informing Colm of Edith's regard for him. She found him snuggly at home, nursing his wounds.

"She's in love with you, Doctor. There's just one problem. She thinks she's too old for you."

His delighted expression fell. "Too old for me?"

"You're...what? Thirty-two?"

"Twenty-eight," he huffed. This girl was not good for his ego.

"Ah, that explains it. She's thirty-five."

"I know. It's on her chart," he added quickly.

"How much does she weigh?"

"A hundred and thirty... that's none of your business!" She giggled uncontrollably until he too gave in to humor.

"Have you decided on your proposal yet?"

"No, I'm still thinking."

"Want some help?"

"No, not yet anyway. I've got a few ideas."

"Alright. Well, I'll let you know if I find out anything else."

He watched her wander down the sidewalk to the street. His heart sank at the movement of the curtains next door.

Edith barely heard the door to the pharmacy closet close as she searched for a bottle of aspirin. Turning, she ran smack into Dr. Byrne and dropped the glass bottle. He caught it just before it hit the floor and blocked her exit.

"I think there's been a misunderstanding."

"About what?" she asked, smiling more brightly than she felt. Goodness, he was handsome! When would she ever get over him?

"I'm not interested in Louisa Musgrave."

"Oh."

He took a step closer. "Someone far more intriguing has caught my eye." His eyes twinkled as he leaned in close. She couldn't look away.

"I...I see. Louisa will be disappointed."

"No, I don't think so."

"No?"

"No."

As she struggled to come up with a response, he placed his hands on her cheeks and tipped her chin up. She let out a soft gasp.

"This woman...I find she quite captivates me," he said. Her lips parted, but no sound came out. His face was within inches of hers. Would he kiss her?

"Doctor!" yelled a voice from the hallway.

Dr. Byrne quickly kissed her forehead before rushing from the closet. He had kissed her forehead. She wasn't sure how to feel about that.

The pharmacy closet was hardly the proper place for a first kiss but kiss her he had...in the same place he might kiss his mother. Around Edith, he was as joint knight in shining armor and court jester. No wonder she misread his signals! On top of that, he'd shortly thereafter invited her on another picnic which he'd had to cancel due to being on call in place of Dr. Vasser. A knock at his office door forced him to remove his face from his hands. Edith stood in the threshold with a concerned look on her face.

"Are you alright, Doctor?"

"No, not really."

She hastened forward, reaching over his desk to touch his forehead, of all places. "You're not feverish. How about I ask Tilly to bring our supper over here?"

The thought of spending the evening alone with Edith sent his heart racing. "I don't think that's a good idea," he managed to choke out.

He almost gave in when her smile drooped. She was precious to him, so precious that he didn't trust himself around her if they were to be alone.

"Alright, if that's what you wish," she said, her long brown eyelashes kissing her cheeks.

"I'll be fine. Hopefully, it will be a quiet evening."

He watched her leave the room, congratulating himself on his godly decision, while wishing with all his heart to hold her in his arms.

Dr. Byrne's manner toward her had changed. His flirtatiousness had been replaced with something more serious, and he seemed unwilling to be too close to her. She shook her head. What a confusing man! Unless she was sorely mistaken, he had feelings for her, but for the life of him, he wouldn't show them. Perhaps he was embarrassed. What would people say? They spent long hours working side by side and dined together frequently. Would people think she'd thrown herself at him?

A few weeks had passed since their encounter in the pharmacy closet. He'd not made a single romantic move since then, but she felt his eyes on her constantly. What was on his mind? She'd rather have out with it than be kept in the dark.

She decided to consult Mrs. Stevens and was just on her way to do so when she saw the doctor exiting the parsonage. He was whistling as he tucked something into his pocket. He turned away from her to head down the lane toward The Tea Biscuit. She decided to continue on her errand rather than spoil his happy mood.

"Dear Edith! This is a pleasant surprise," cried Mrs. Stevens, pulling her into a hug. "To what do I owe this pleasure?"

"I'm hoping for some advice."

"Well, well. I'll do my best. Would you like some tea?"

"No, but thank you. I don't think I could eat a bite at the moment."

They settled in the cozy parlor, and Mrs. Stevens motioned to Edith to have out with her concerns.

"It's a matter of the heart, Mrs. Stevens."

"Ah. The heart is a very fickle thing, never being sure of what it wants."

"How do you mean?"

"As you know, the Bible tells us to follow our head, not our heart. The heart can go off on a whim which the head would never go."

"Yes, you are right."

"What is it, my dear?" Mrs. Stevens asked, patting Edith's hand.

"I love him," Edith blurted out, long withheld tears tumbling down her cheeks.

"Who?"

"Dr. Byrne."

The preacher's wife pulled her into her arms and held her while she cried out all her pent up feelings. When Edith finally leaned back, Mrs. Stevens handed her a clean handkerchief.

"So, you find yourself in love with the doctor, and this knowledge brings you to tears." It wasn't said in condemnation but rather a statement of fact. Edith nodded miserably and blew her nose.

"I don't know...what to do. I thought at first he was just flirting, and then when I believed him to be in love with Louisa, I was torn between jealousy and happiness for her. Well, he's not in love with her, and he seemed to return my affections, but now he's grown...distant."

The good lady sat patiently while Edith contemplated her feelings. Then, she grasped Edith's hand and squeezed it.

"Edith, in cases like this, you have to trust God's timing. I know losing Roger was very hard for you and now your father as well."

"I never expected to feel like this again, and with a younger man, no less. What interest could he really have in me?"

"You are a beautiful and godly woman, my dear, and you're still young. You have much to offer a husband. What is seven years between you if he's the one God's chosen for you?"

"But *has* God chosen him for me? My heart says *yes*, but my head questions everything."

"Shall we pray about this?"

"Yes, please." They bowed their heads, and Mrs. Stevens led them in prayer.

"Most Holy Heavenly Father, only you know what's best for these two dear souls. Lead them to the future you want them to have, whether it be together in love or apart in friendship. Comfort my dear sister Edith, and give her peace and guidance as she makes decisions about her future. In your Son's name, we pray. Amen."

Edith left the parsonage with a light heart and a high step. God's will was best and would prevail. If He wanted her to become Mrs. Byrne, he would open that door. If not, she would await even more wonderful promises in service to her Lord and the patients of Harriford Grange Clinic.

Colm held the ring up to the light. The modest diamond chip would have to do for now, until he could afford something larger. It sparkled brilliantly in the morning sun, throwing a rainbow of colors on the stark walls of his office. He placed it back in its box and slipped it into his desk drawer.

After visiting the jeweler, he'd spent a long time with Mr. Stevens. The preacher had listened patiently, prayed with him, and sent him away encouraged. He now felt he could move forward with his plan. He smiled to himself as he pictured the ring on Edith's slim finger and her hand clasped in his. When she knocked on his office door to ask about one of their patients, he rose calmly and strode toward her. As he answered her question, he noticed the serenity of her countenance and the light of her smile. On an impulse, he bent down and kissed her cheek. He relished in her blush as he left her to tend to Mr. Robertson's gout.

Saturday dawned with a pleasant crispness. Edith opened her front door to find Dr. Byrne on the other side, clad in his finest suit and carrying a picnic basket.

"Good morning, Miss Caldwell! Would you do me the honor of accompanying me on a picnic?"

She curtsied dramatically. "I would be honored, Dr. Byrne...Colm."

A comfortable ease had blanketed their friendship since her talk with Mrs. Stevens. She smiled at the pleasure in his eyes as she used his given name. After grabbing her shawl and parasol, she took his arm, and they set off.

No one was about while they set out their meal, a delicious spread catered by The Tea Biscuit. They talked of their medical practice, church affairs, and the fine weather until they were stuffed. After cleaning up, Colm held out his hand.

"Will you take a walk with me?" He held onto her hand as they walked, intertwining his fingers with hers.

"I love this place," she whispered when they stopped by some small rapids.

"And I love you."

She pivoted toward him as he put his arm around her.

"I love you too," she breathed. Looking up at him, she prepared for a kiss, but it didn't come. Instead, he dropped to one knee and pulled out a small velvet box. He opened it to reveal a gold band set with a sparkling diamond.

"Edith Caldwell, love of my life and queen of my heart, will you marry me?"

She covered her mouth as a happy tear slid from her eye.

"Yes, most definitely yes!"

He slipped the ring onto her finger and stood to take her in his arms. She tipped her face up again, and this time, she was rewarded with his kiss, full of love and promises.

Walking back to their picnic blanket, she reflected on the power of perception. She'd made assumptions which were untrue based on what she perceived rather than on the facts. She resolved never to give in to such thoughts but to diligently search for the truth. The light of love shone brightly on this new chapter of her life, and she thanked God that Dr. Colm Byrne had come to the practice at Harriford Grange. By her fiancé's grin, she knew he was thinking the very same thing.

The Farrier's Girl

"Have you heard *who* the new farrier is?" Mrs. Bowman asked the other ladies gathered in The Tea Biscuit, the most popular restaurant in Harriford Grange. She raised her gray eyebrows high over her tea cup. "Ian Tiffany from Blaketon Commons!"

Gasps flew out of mouths all around twenty-two-year-old Louisa Musgrave. She leaned over to her mother. "Who is Ian Tiffany?"

"The new farrier, apparently," Lady Musgrave responded with a half smile.

"Mother!"

"So," asked Mrs. Pickford, "Moira Tiffany's son thinks he'll be welcome in Harriford Grange. How disgraceful! I wouldn't have him so much as muck out my stalls as to lay a single finger on one of my fine steeds."

"And what, pray tell, is his offense?" asked Louisa's mother.

Faces reddened as the other ladies looked at each other. "How could you not have heard, Lady Musgrave? It was all over at the time," replied Mrs. Bowman, leaning forward eagerly.

Her mother shifted uncomfortably. "You all know how I detest gossip…"

"Is it gossip if it's true?" asked Louisa, wanting to know what all the fuss over Ian Tiffany was about.

"Louisa…"

"The girl's right, you know. It is true."

"What's true?"

"Louisa, I think it's time to…"

"Ian Tiffany is a…"

"She never married!" Mrs. Pickford blurted out, not wanting to hear that awful word. "Moira Tiffany and his father…they never married!"

"Come, Louisa. We're not going to listen to these gossips a moment longer!"

Louisa allowed her reticule to slip from her fingers and took longer than necessary to retrieve it. The ladies were enjoying the scathing tale of Moira Tiffany's indiscretion too much to be affronted by her mother's piety.

"Who was his father?" asked Miss Dickenson.

"A gypsy!"

"No!"

"Have you seen him? He didn't get those dark locks from Moira!"

"They say he seduced her…and left town the next day, never to be heard from again."

The bell on the door clanged soundly as her mother slammed it behind them. Louisa trotted to keep up with her mother's rage.

"Don't you pay any attention to those gossips, Louisa! Your father says Ian Tiffany is a fine young man and an excellent farrier, and we're fortunate to have him coming so soon to Rosewood Manor."

"What they said, though…is it true? Is Ian a…"

Her mother huffed and swung toward her.

"I don't know, but listen to me very carefully, young lady. Whether the story about Moira Tiffany's boy is true or not, he will always be welcome in our home. Now, I don't want to hear another word about this."

"Mother...Mother!"

Louisa peeked into the hallway to study the young man talking with her father. He was short for a man, about equal to her five-foot-seven-and-a-half-inch frame, but he more than made up for that in looks. Thick jet black hair complimented his swarthy complexion, reminding her of a character from one of her adventure novels. He was muscular and plainly, but cleanly, dressed. He must be another one of her father's hospitality projects.

As an elder in the church, Lord Peter Musgrave, who detested the title required by his rank, took the Bible's charge of hospitality seriously. One never knew who would be invited to dine at Rosewood from one week to the next. She put on her sweetest smile and approached the man from behind, catching her father's eye for an introduction.

"Ah, Louisa! There you are, my love," her father announced jovially.

The young man turned toward her, his expression pleasant and as handsome as expected. His most striking feature, however, was the vivid cerulean color of his eyes. She was at a loss for words, which for Louisa Musgrave was a very rare occurrence indeed. She smiled intriguingly at her father as the exotic stranger bowed low over her hand.

"It's a pleasure to make your acquaintance, Miss Musgrave."

Her father stepped forward with a delighted grin. "Louisa, this is Ian Tiffany, the new farrier."

"Ian...Tiffany?" she repeated, her smile fading into shock. She pulled her hand from his and looked at him with a newfound dislike. Well, that explained his looks. "I see. Charmed, I'm sure." She curtsied quickly, almost throwing herself off balance and hustled toward the door of the dining room. She knew her parents' detested discrimination, but this guest was a new low, even for the goodness of Lord and Lady Musgrave.

Ian brushed off Lord Musgrave's apologies with feigned indifference. Should he be surprised that the "delightful" Miss Musgrave didn't think any more of him than any other young woman? He motioned to his cousin Tilly Grant, who took his arm and accompanied him into the dining room.

Much to his dismay, he was seated next to Miss Musgrave. Tilly was much better off, having been assigned to sit by the widowered butcher Mr. Thomas Wilcox. He was sure he would have had a much better chance of interesting conversation with that gentleman than the sullen-faced blonde beside him.

"Mr. Tiffany," Miss Musgrave said icily, "would you please pass the salt?"

Ian grabbed the salt shaker and plopped it down unceremoniously next to her plate. The cut glass vial swayed back and forth before toppling over. He bit his lip in both embarrassment and to keep from laughing as they scrambled to set it aright. Salt streamed out like water from a rock all over the young woman's creamed potatoes. The look in her eyes could have killed.

"Mandy," cried Lady Musgrave to the maid, "please bring Miss Musgrave a new plate!"

The other diners happily recommenced their conversations while a storm cloud brewed over their little corner.

"My apologies, Miss Musgrave, truly."

"Humph!"

Later, in the drawing room…

"Louisa, the light outside is still good for another hour. Why don't you take Miss Grant and Mr. Tiffany out to the maze?" her father suggested.

As Louisa scrambled to come up with an excuse, Miss Grant begged off, saying she was too tired for a romp through the maze. Relieved, Louisa started to sit down on the needlepoint chair.

"I'm sure Mr. Tiffany would like a go at it," said her mother.

"It would hardly be proper, my lady," replied Mr. Tiffany. Louisa heartily agreed.

"Nonsense, my boy. On the contrary, I think you might find it most enjoyable," Lord Musgrave replied, sneaking a sly look at his wife.

"But...but..." cried Louisa.

Their protests ignored, the two of them found themselves outside the door of the maze accompanied by a manservant. He bowed slightly and stationed himself at the entrance with no intention of following them.

"There you are, Mr. Tiffany," Louisa declared haughtily. "I wish you the best of luck."

He stopped her from leaving, his strong fingers gripping her slim wrist. "Oh no, you don't," he seethed. "If I'm going in there, you're coming with me."

"And why should I do that?"

"You know the way out, don't you?"

"Of course."

"Well...I'm not staying in there all night."

At that moment, he looked vaguely like a lost little boy. He let go of her wrist and offered her his arm. "Accompany me, Miss Musgrave?"

She resigned herself to her fate and took his arm, despairing that she would somehow forget the path through the maze. She needn't have worried. They completed the maze in less than half an hour, emerging on the side nearest the stables.

"Which one's yours?" Ian asked in an attempt to break the icy façade of the fair girl. If he was to work here, he must try to get along with her.

"Flight of Fancy, the chestnut mare halfway down on the left." She made no move to follow him.

"Would you care to show me?"

She huffed before stomping past him and standing like a queen in front of one of the stalls. Inside, a small chestnut mare with a flaxen mane munched happily on some alfalfa hay. Her expression softened as she leaned over to brush her forelock. Ian watched her, feeling himself drawn to her fairy-like beauty. His fingers itched to stroke *her* flaxen locks, but he refrained, fancying it wouldn't be worth the slap he'd likely receive.

"Miss Musgrave," the manservant called, "it's growing dark. You'll be wanted back at the house."

"Thank you, John." She patted Fancy one last time before turning sharply. The heel of her shoe caught in the hem of her satin gown, and before he could catch her, she'd fallen to the wood-chip covered floor.

As Ian scrambled to help her to her feet, he noticed a dark mass right under her empire waistline. Looking closer, he saw that she'd fallen right into a pile of horse droppings. As she slowly stood up, mortification cloaked her features. Her gown, as far as he could tell, was ruined.

"Are you alright, Miss Musgrave?"

She gritted her teeth. "Does it look like I'm alright, Mr. Tiffany?" With a look of pure disgust, she picked off the larger chunks and threw them to the floor. He barely refrained from laughing, knowing it was hardly what she wanted to hear. Back at the main house, she fled from him though the foyer and started up the grand staircase.

"Oh my, Louisa! What on earth has happened to you?" her mother asked, aghast at the hideous sight her daughter now made. For some reason, Louisa looked at him before answering.

"I fell."

"Dear me! Upstairs at once. I'll send for Penny."

Lord Musgrave made further inquiries from Ian and John, who thankfully was there to prove Ian's innocence in the matter. Tilly and Mr. Wilcox exchanged a few words before Ian claimed her arm and escorted her home.

The next morning, Ian brushed his buckskin-hued hand over the flank of Jupiter, Lord Musgrave's favorite steed. The Friesian stallion was a fine specimen – black as midnight with a spirit of fire. At seventeen and a half hands, he stood taller than Ian's five-foot-seven frame and over most of the other horses in the Rosewood Stud. He leaned against the stallion who lifted his hoof obligingly.

"Good boy," Ian cooed. He'd always loved horses. They never failed to lift his spirits...and they never judged him. He proceeded to remove the horseshoe and trim off excess growth. He'd finished filing the toe smooth when he heard movement within the doorway. He allowed Jupiter to set his foot down before peering around the stallion's silky tail. He groaned within himself. What was *she* doing out here? He turned back to his work. If he was lucky, she'd leave him in peace.

"Mr. Tiffany!"

No such luck. He considered ignoring her, but his respect for her mother and father ran too deep. He set down his rasp, and taking care to touch the stallion, he rounded his rump and stopped in front of Miss Musgrave.

"Miss." He stood eye-to-eye with the young woman. "Did the stain come out?"

She scowled at him. He shouldn't have said that. He knew better, but this one…she got under his skin like no other woman. He bowed his head contritely.

"Forgive my rudeness. What can I do for you, Miss Musgrave?"

"Have you finished with Fancy yet?"

"First thing this morning, miss."

"Very good."

He eyed her luxurious blue velvet riding habit. It set off her wavy golden hair and steel gray eyes.

"Would you like me to saddle her for you or find one of the grooms?"

"No, thank you, Mr. Tiffany. I'm *quite capable* of tacking her up myself."

She pushed past him and made a beeline for Flight of Fancy's stall. As he watched her ridiculous outfit swish behind her, he heard a rumble of thunder. He hastened to look out into the flawlessly blue sky. He glanced at the trees. The birds were restless.

"Miss Musgrave," he called, hurrying back into the barn. "Miss Musgrave, I think you'd best put off your riding for the morning. It looks like a storm's coming."

She looked at him as if he'd sprouted wings.

"Nonsense. Have you looked outside? It's a perfect day for a ride." Using her dainty arms, she hefted her sidesaddle over the chestnut mare's back and hastened to take up the cinch. He put his calloused hand over hers. Daggers shot from her pupils. "Please remove your hand, sir."

He lowered his hand but remained where he was. "It looks it now, but I heard thunder, and the birds are restless."

Her tinkling laugh might have charmed him if it wasn't exuded in haughty disgust. "The birds are restless, Mr. Tiffany? I never heard the like of it."

"Miss Musgrave, surely you would err on caution."

"Indeed, sir, if caution were needed. However, it is not, and I *am* going to ride." She pulled the cinch tight and double-checked her work. He stood between her and the bridle.

"Miss Musgrave, I must insist..."

Her grey eyes took on a becomingly demure look which sent warning bells reverberating through him. She stepped close and tapped her chin thoughtfully. What was the vixen up to?

"Mr. Tiffany," she drawled, "is it true what they say?"

"What who say?" he replied through barred teeth.

"About your parents..." She smirked when his unusually blue eyes grew dark. "I'll be having my ride now, sir, if you'll excuse me." She reached past him for her bridle, her soft hair brushing his cheek. He stalked out of the stall. Foolish girl! But he'd warned her. He'd warned her.

"Insufferable man!" Louisa seethed, nudging Fancy into a canter. The forest loomed before her, and she rushed into its shelter. After his antics last night, how could Mother and Father keep him on? He'd embarrassed her and made her the laughingstock of the evening! And her dress was ruined, through and through. She vowed never to forgive him.

After riding for half an hour, her anger abated, and her conscience pricked her. What was she thinking, embarrassing him like that? It wasn't his fault what his parents had done. But, oh, how he irked her! It was worth it just to see him squirm. From day one, he'd had no use for her, writing her off as a spoiled brat. They were both Christians. He even intended to start attending the church at Harriford Grange at her parents' invitation. So why did he assume the worst about her? *Why do you assume the worst about him?* She pulled her mare to a stop. She should apologize.

As she turned Fancy toward home, a bright flash lit the sky. She'd been so distracted that she hadn't noticed the growing darkness. She raced out of the forest. He'd been right. A storm had come. She was just about to cross the stone bridge when another flash slashed the sky in two. A deafening roar shook the ground beneath Fancy's hooves. Frightened, she reared. Unable to maintain her balance, Louisa tumbled from her back and hit the ground. The world around her went black.

Ian and the grooms rushed about the paddock, pulling horses into the safety of the barn. This was no ordinary thunderstorm. He rushed to Fancy's stall. It was empty. He grabbed the nearest hand.

"Where's Fancy?"

"Haven't seen her."

"Miss Musgrave took her out about an hour ago."

"Maybe she went to the house."

Ian darted into the driving rain to find Fancy galloping toward him, her saddle eerily empty. He grabbed her reins, patting her reassuringly while hurrying her into the barn. Handing her off, he ran out again, searching the drive for any sign of Louisa. He followed the path she'd taken until he reached the stone bridge. His heart stopped beating when he caught sight of a pile of blue velvet, soaked through from the rain. He ran to her and patted her cheek.

"Miss Musgrave! Louisa! Miss Musgrave!" No response. He threw his oilskin coat over them both and put his hand to her throat. It was faint, but there was a pulse. He cupped her porcelain cheek in his hand, but she still didn't stir. Throwing back his coat, he waved frantically at the barn and caught the eye of one of the grooms.

"Call the doctor! Miss Musgrave's injured!" As soon as the boy ran to fetch the doctor, Ian fell beside Louisa and grasped her hand in his. "Forgive me, Miss Musgrave. Please forgive me."

Dr. and Mrs. Byrne supervised the removal of Louisa to the main house. Ian paced outside her bedroom door, yearning for news, and yet knowing he couldn't be nearer to her. He raised bloodshot eyes as her father exited the room.

"How is she?" Ian asked.

Lord Musgrave sank onto a settee and buried his face in his hands. Ian fell down beside him.

"She's still unconscious. Dr. Byrne says her brain is swelling."

"Is she going to…?" No, he couldn't bring himself to say it.

"It's a waiting game, he says. Unless it goes down by the morning, she may suffer irreparable damage…or worse."

Ian rose and threw his wadded up cap to the floor. "I told her not to go! I tried to warn her. I knew a storm was coming. I warned her, but she wouldn't listen!" When her father didn't respond, he sat back down. "I should have stopped her. We had words, and I was angry with her. But I should have stopped her. I'm so sorry, sir. This is all my fault." He gripped his raven-black hair with his hands, but he didn't shed a tear. He'd learned long ago that tears got a man nothing but trouble. But for the first time in a long time, he sure wished he could cry.

Lord Musgrave took in the sight of the young man hunched next to him. He'd been fond of the farrier since first meeting him. Not one to insist upon a marriage within her class, he'd hoped Louisa would take an interest in him, but so far, they seemed to hate each other. *Well, until now, that is.*

"Son, it wasn't your fault. My daughter is a spirited young lady, and if she has her mind set on something, well, there's not much a man can do to stop her."

"I should have taken her bridle when I had a chance."

"She would have found another. Ian, I know my daughter, and she wouldn't blame you, and for what it's worth, I don't believe the good Lord blames you either."

Ian pondered this for a moment before thanking him. "May I…May I see her, sir?"

Lord Musgrave stood and motioned to the door. "Right this way."

Her skin held a deathly pallor, and Ian shuddered at the thought. Mrs. Byrne, the doctor's wife, touched a handkerchief to her eye before holding out her hand to him. He moved up next to the bed and dared to touch Louisa's hand. Lord Musgrave made no move to stop him. He knelt down as the others left the room.

"Miss Musgrave…Louisa…if you can hear me…please forgive me for…for…everything."

He gazed upon her, drinking in her fair beauty. Her long golden waves were spread about her delicate face. A passing thought of *Sleeping Beauty* came to him, and he wished he were the prince who could break the spell and awaken her from her slumber. He slid his finger along her cheek and found himself leaning closer. He pulled back and chided himself. That would never be. Even if she were under a spell, he was by no means a prince.

The Musgrave household kept watch through the night, but Louisa made no move to stir from her slumber. Her father rarely left her side, and her mother, never. Edith Byrne urged Mrs. Musgrave to take a rest, but she could not be prevailed upon to leave her daughter. Mr. Musgrave was pleased that Edith had found love again after losing his son Roger. It was an answer to prayer. Constant prayer was being offered for Louisa, and he hoped God would answer it with equal favor.

When Ian had appeared early in the morning, Lord Musgrave knew the boy hadn't slept a wink. Was it simply misplaced guilt, or were deeper feelings at play? Would he ever know? He bowed his head and sent up another heartfelt plea for his darling Louisa.

Ian returned to his work, but his heart wasn't in it. He went through the motions and even made fair progress on the Rosewood Stud, but something inside him had changed. Louisa Musgrave consumed his thoughts, and he realized why she'd irked him so. Of all the women he'd met, he'd never longed for their notice or approval until Louisa. Instead of opening his heart to her, he'd thrown up a wall and pushed her away. No wonder she'd reacted so harshly.

And then there was the matter of his birth. Since his youngest days, a shadow had plagued him. After having been seduced by an unscrupulous traveling man, his mother had found herself with child. She had died in childbirth, leaving him in the care of his aunt in Blaketon Commons. Was twenty-six years of good Christian conduct not enough to rid him of the stigma? He leaned his head against the bay mare he was shoeing and breathed in her scent. Horse – hay, sweat, and whatever else. He always found it comforting at times like this. He sent up another prayer for Louisa, deep and heartfelt, and feeling a little encouraged, he went back to work.

Louisa's eyelids fluttered open, and she started at the sight around her. Where was she? Who were these people? What was going on? Her head ached as names and places slowly drifted back to her. Her mother put a settling hand on her shoulder.

"Stay still, my love. You took quite a tumble yesterday."

Edith felt of her forehead and reached for a damp cloth. It was cool and refreshing against her skin, but she was still alarmed.

"What…happened?"

"You fell from Fancy during the storm yesterday and hit your head," her mother answered. "We were very worried about you last night, but it seems you're going to be alright after all."

"The swelling has gone down," reported Edith, smiling at Louisa. "You'll need rest for a few days, and we'll need to watch for any signs of brain damage. However, it seems like you're healing very well."

"How's Fancy?"

"She's fine. Mr. Tiffany's been taking special care of her," her mother replied.

"Ian? Ian Tiffany?"

"Yes. He feels responsible for your accident."

Closing her eyes, she remembered his warnings…and her defiant disregard.

"It's not his fault."

"We know."

"Can you tell him, Mother? Tell him it's not his fault!"

They settled her back with strict orders to not move.

"Please, Mother," she repeated, "tell him it's not his fault."

"I will, my darling. Now you get some rest and maybe in a little while, we can see about something to eat."

A week later at Louisa's request, Ian was summoned to her room. Mrs. Byrne sat quietly in one corner knitting something small and pink and pretending she wasn't listening. Louisa reached out to him timidly, and he placed his hand in hers. It did him much good to see her awake and smiling again. He sat down in the bedside chair and leaned unreservedly on the mattress.

"How are you feeling?" he whispered. Her dove gray eyes looked out under blonde eyelashes, making his heart skip.

"Much better," she murmured. "I wanted to tell you...the day I fell...I wanted to tell you I was sorry. I said some terrible things to you. Please forgive me."

"If you'll forgive me..."

She nodded and shifted toward him. Mrs. Byrne stole a glance, but after determining they were not up to anything improper, she went back to her knitting.

"I forgive you. Ian, did you visit me while I was asleep?"

"Yes."

She ran her fingertips absentmindedly over his hand, making it hard to concentrate on her words. "I heard you. I don't remember anything else, but I remember that."

They held each other's gaze for a long moment. He searched for a sign of her regard, but finding nothing conclusive, he looked away.

"Let's start over," she suggested, drawing his eyes back to her. She smiled brightly and held out her hand. "Hello! My name is Louisa Musgrave. What's yours?"

Laughing softly, he shook her hand. "Ian Tiffany."

"It's a pleasure to meet you, Mr. Tiffany."

"Ian, please."

"And you may call me Louisa. Now, see? We're friends already."

Emboldened by her rapport, he kissed her hand. "If you wish...Louisa." He enjoyed the rosy blush which accompanied her surprised smile.

"Enough of that, young man," called Mrs. Byrne in a teasing tone. "She's not quite ready for romancing!"

Louisa giggled uncontrollably as his face turned scarlet, but her hand still clinging to his told him she might not object to being romanced by him after all.

The following Sunday morning when Louisa was well recovered, she looked for Ian at the worship service. Seeing him sitting in the back row, she motioned him to her.

"Please sit with us."

"I'm not sure that's a good idea," he hedged.

She grabbed his arm, catching him off guard, and nudged him to her normal pew. "You saved my life. The least I can do is ask you to sit with me." When he looked around uncertainly, she gently turned his face back to hers. "Ian, we're friends now. I don't care about your past. I want to be with you...and be seen with you."

She hoped he caught the subtle meaning in her words. If he did, he didn't show it, but at least he acquiesced to her request and seated himself on the pew with her.

"You're too far away. It looks like you think I have the plague."

Blushing, he scooted closer but not enough to touch.

"That's better."

"Should I put my arm around you as well?" he whispered.

"If you wish," she teased, hoping he might follow through. He shook his head and muttered something. "What was that? I didn't hear you."

His only response was a wink, but it sent happy jitters straight to her heart. She struggled to turn her attention to the service. Mr. Stevens chose this morning to preach on the subject of prejudice and the destruction it could cause. As she reflected on God's equality toward mankind, she thought of how she'd treated Ian. She'd listened to gossip and allowed it to taint the way she'd looked at him. She didn't see him for the person he was but as a product of circumstances beyond his control. She brushed away a tear and looked at Ian. He had a similar look of remorse on his face. Had he been guilty of prejudice too?

When Mr. Stevens offered the invitation, Louisa started toward the aisle but was stopped by Ian. He gripped her hand, and together they went to sit on the front pew. Each shared in a note to the congregation how they had allowed themselves to become blinded by prejudice and had showed this in a public manner. Specifics weren't asked, but forgiveness was given. Louisa left the service with a lightness of spirit.

Her parents accepted a luncheon invitation from Mr. and Mrs. Stevens, but Louisa begged off. Ian seemed hesitant to leave her side and she, his. She obtained permission for the two of them to dine at The Tea Biscuit. Inside, she chose a table by the window and looked about for the normal crowd of gossips.

"Who are you looking for?" Ian asked.

She reddened sheepishly. "There's a group of ladies Mother and I used to meet for tea who...were gossiping about you. I suppose I wanted them to see us together," she added defiantly.

He reached across the table to clasp her hand. "Don't worry about them anymore. God wouldn't want you to trouble yourself about such things. And neither do I."

They ordered a full spread and were soon too absorbed in each other to notice the gossips whispering in the corner. Leaving the restaurant arm in arm, they wandered leisurely down the lane with no particular destination in mind.

"I have a confession to make," Ian said, casting a sly glance her way.

"Oh?" she replied, arching a brow.

"I had a talk with your father the other day."

Her heart fluttered wildly, like a bird wishing to be set free. "What did you discuss?"

"I asked him if he would allow me to court his daughter."

"I see. What did he say?"

"He approved...on one condition."

"What condition?"

"That his daughter accept me."

She paused in the lane and turned coyly toward him. "Have you asked her yet?"

"I was hoping to. I was waiting for the right time."

"Well, I think it's that time."

Grinning, he took both of her hands in his and looked her in the eye. "Miss Louisa Musgrave, just when I thought I couldn't stand you, you were wiling your way into my heart. I've come to love you, truly and deeply. It would mean everything to me if you would accept me."

Stepping closer, she thrilled when he put his arms around her. Looking into his loving blue eyes, she bent forward and gave him a light kiss. His surprise was replaced with a look of joy untold.

"Is that a yes?" he asked, nuzzling her nose with his.

"What do you think?" she whispered, kissing him again. This time, he held her a little longer before tucking her hand into the crook of his arm.

"You still haven't said *yes*, you know," he teased.

"On the contrary," she volleyed back, "I believe I've said *yes* a thousand times over."

He tugged her forward, leading her toward a future bright with possibilities. What lay ahead, she didn't know, but with God and Ian by her side, she knew she would be the happiest woman on earth.

The Butcher's Lady

"I've been waiting for you, Matilda." The deep, now familiar voice sent chills up her spine. How could she have ever thought he was handsome? The porcelain tea cup rattled in her hand, forcing her to set it back onto the silver tray.

"Please forgive me. I was delayed. Mrs. Byrne needed help with something," Tilly Grant responded, willing her voice to be confident. "But I'm here now. I'll just take this tray to your mother."

Strong hands settled on her slim hips and pulled her small frame backwards. His breath warmed her neck, and she turned instinctively away. He pushed his face into her thick red hair and breathed deeply.

"Lilacs. It suits you perfectly."

"Thank you," she replied, knowing resistance was futile. She'd attempted that yesterday and lost. "I'm sure your mother is waiting for me."

Reluctantly, he released her and stepped back. "You can't run forever, Matilda," he replied. "Mother loves having you around almost as much as I do."

She took a moment to compose herself before carrying the brimming tea tray to Mrs. Kerrington. She'd agreed to assist Edith in caring for the elderly church member long before Lucas Kerrington moved back to town.

Now that Edith was in her seventh month, thirty-two-year-old Tilly was alone. She shifted the tray to one hand before opening the door to the good lady's bedroom. At least in her presence, Tilly would have some peace.

Thomas Wilcox hefted the heavy cleaver and brought it down on the shoulder of the pig's carcass in front of him. Deftly separating the joints, he placed the meat in the cooler and surveyed his work. They were all set for the next day. Washing his hands, he let his thoughts wander to their usual abode.

With her rich auburn hair and lively green eyes, Tilly Grant was the picture of perfection. Her petite frame and spunky demeanor had captured his heart since first talking with her at the Musgraves' dinner several months ago. He looked forward to her daily stops in the butcher shop like he did the molten fudge cake at The Tea Biscuit.

After losing Sally ten years before to consumption, forty-year-old Thomas thought he would never love another woman. She had been the light of his world, and with her death, that light had gone out. He ran a clean hand through his thinning dark brown hair and closed his brown eyes. Sally would have liked her, and he knew she would want him to move on. If only he could.

The bell over the shop door rang, bringing with it the lady herself. He watched her tired eyes search the room, and he stepped up to the counter.

"Evening, Miss Grant! How may I help you?"

"Good evening, Mr. Wilcox. A ham and a beef roast, please." She put a pretty hand over her yawn. "Oh my! Excuse me!"

He smiled at her and began to prepare her order. Within minutes, their transaction was complete, and Miss Tilly Grant was yet another happy memory. He shook his head at his own shyness. *She doesn't even know I exist.*

Lucas Kerrington bent toward the gilt framed mirror in the foyer and smoothed his blonde mustache. Ever since his return to this backwater town, he'd spent his days in perpetual boredom. That is, except when Matilda Grant was around. *Tilly*, as she preferred, had caught his eye, and even though she was much too poor to marry, he enjoyed toying with her. She was much better company than Bernice Ralston, his fiancée. Bernice wasn't due to arrive for a fortnight, leaving him plenty of time for Matilda.

Movement outside caught his eye, and he spent several minutes watching Matilda walk up the drive to the servants' entrance. Her frumpy brown dress was all wrong for her petite figure. He made a mental note to rectify that as soon as possible.

"Oh, Mr. Kerrington, I didn't see you there!" Tilly exclaimed, backing away. He reached for her hand and put it to his lips.

"My dear Matilda, you must know by now how much I admire you."

She nodded her head, keeping her eyes on the floor. He wrapped his arm around her waist and pulled her close. She put up her hands and pushed against his chest.

"Really, sir, I don't think..."

"Just one kiss, Matilda."

"Please, Mr. Kerrington, let me go," she replied, fighting tears.

"Lucas," he whispered, his lips brushing her ear.

"Lucas, please let me go."

"Is that you, Tilly?" called an elderly female voice.

"Yes, Mrs. Kerrington. I'll be there in a moment."

He relinquished his hold on her, and she fled to the kitchen. He was getting more forceful each day. She wanted to help Mrs. Kerrington, but how much longer would she be able to resist him? She bent her head and prayed that God would intervene and save her from Lucas Kerrington's advances.

Thomas watched Tilly as she stared at the meat case. Her mind was miles away. Even he could see that.

"Miss Grant?"

"Hm?"

"Miss Grant, are you...are you alright?" He leaned over the counter and tried to catch her attention. She looked up at him with eyes red from crying. "Something wrong, miss?"

She waved her hand. "Oh no, Mr. Wilcox. I'm quite well. Thank you."

He knit his eyebrows until she looked away embarrassed. "I'm sorry, Miss Grant. What can I get for you today?"

"I don't know. What do you suggest?"

My shoulder to cry on. "The pork shoulder is quite nice today."

"Alright."

He observed her as he wrapped up her order. The bright, bubbly Miss Grant hadn't been around for almost a week. Something was wrong, but how would he ever find out what it was? A man who spent his days covered in blood wasn't exactly attractive to women.

"Miss Grant?"

"Yes?"

"That Mrs. Byrne, she's got a good ear on her if you need someone to talk to."

"Thank you, Mr. Wilcox. I appreciate that. Well, good day."

He watched her slump-shouldered figure wander toward home. *Heavenly Father, please comfort that young woman and guide me to a way I can help her. In Jesus' name, Amen.*

Lucas opened the package and pulled out the blue silk readymade gown he'd bought from the shop in town. He'd said it was for his cousin. Funny thing, he had no cousin. He traced the low neckline with his fingers and imagined Matilda wearing it. She would look ravishing. He showed it to his mother who, in her childlike innocence, took to the idea with relish. His logic? If Mother gave the girl the dress, she would be obliged to wear it.

As planned, Matilda changed into the elegant gown shortly after arriving. Lucas' senile mother had given her no choice. *What a delight it would be to see a pretty young girl dressed for a ball again!* she'd cooed. It really was a much better option for the beautiful young woman. He sat leisurely by the fireplace, watching her bustle uncomfortably about the room. Almost off the shoulder and a little too tight, the gown gave him a pleasure which Beatrice's stuffy dresses never did. He waited impatiently for his chance to get her alone.

Tilly worked as efficiently as the suffocating gown would allow. Mrs. Kerrington would never have thought to buy her a dress. It had to be Lucas' work, and in order to keep her promise to help Edith, she had to go along with it…didn't she? She shuddered as his eyes searched her form. How far would he take this little charade?

Mrs. Kerrington began to snore, signaling to Tilly that it was time to remove the tea tray. She hurried from the room, hoping foolishly that Lucas wouldn't follow her. After setting the tray in the kitchen, she turned to find him in the doorway.

"Mr. Kerrington?"

"It fits you perfectly," he said with a wicked grin.

She backed into the counter and sidled toward the other exit. "It's a lovely gown. I...I've never seen another more lovely."

He caught her by the hand and put his other hand on the small of her back. "I'm glad you like it." He guided her through the butler's pantry to the parlor and closed the doors. "Now that my mother is asleep, I thought we might like to be better acquainted."

She stumbled and fell back onto a damask settee, and he was by her side in a moment. "Mr. Kerrington, please! This is hardly appropriate. Someone might come along." Indeed, she hoped someone would.

"No, my dear," he said, kissing her hand and then her arm. "No one is coming. You're all mine this afternoon." He moved in closer and began to kiss her bare shoulder. She let out a terrified gasp, but it only seemed to fuel his ardor. He gripped her around the waist and put his mouth to her neck. She clawed at him and screamed, but no one came to her rescue. What would she do if he went further?

"I'll tell your mother what you've done!" she threatened.

"She'll never believe you."

"I'll tell the police!"

"You wouldn't dare." He pulled away from her neck and glared at her with his cold slate blue eyes. Drawing a folding knife from his pocket, he slowly opened the blade and let it glint in the light. She shook her head. He stuffed it back in his pocket. His fire for her having cooled, he stood. Pulling her to her feet, he raked his eyes over her once more. "Mother will be awaking soon."

She hurried back to Mrs. Kerrington's room determined not to reveal what had happened to the sweet older lady. Once released from the gown and Lucas Kerrington's attentions, she allowed all of her tears to fall.

What was she to do? Was helping good Mrs. Kerrington really worth enduring this?

Her eyes were red and puffy again. Thomas went around the counter and put his hand on her elbow.

"Miss Grant, are you feeling well?" She jumped away from him like a mouse from a cat. Her hand went to her throat, and she laughed unconvincingly.

"Dear me, Mr. Wilcox, you frightened me! I'm afraid I've been somewhere else these last few minutes."

He followed her to the other side of the shop and bent down to her level. Laying his hand lightly on her shoulder, he started to speak when he noticed a distinctive red mark just below her hairline. He'd only seen one other woman with marks like that, and that woman had been his wife. Eyes widening, Miss Grant pulled her collar up and stepped away.

"I...I don't think I want anything today after all." As she scurried from the shop, he was once more reminded of a terrified mouse. The Tilly Grant he knew was no mouse. He called out to his assistant and threw off his apron. Minutes later, he was at the clinic waiting not so patiently to see Dr. Colm Byrne.

"Doctor," Thomas said, shaking his hand.

Dr. Byrne motioned to the other chair in the office, and Thomas fell into it. "What's on your mind, Thomas?"

"It's Miss Grant, sir. I...I think she may be in trouble."

"Why do you think that?"

Thomas closed his eyes and willed his racing heart to still. If he was going to help Tilly, he had to calm down. Once quiet, he related to the doctor the things he'd noticed about her. Her change in behavior, her crying, and of course, the distinctive red mark. Dr. Byrne was silent for a long moment.

"Who do you think is behind this?"

"I don't know, sir. It's just that, see, she comes by the shop almost every day, and well, a fellow just notices things."

"You care a lot about her, don't you?" Thomas reddened and dropped his head. Dr. Byrne cleared his throat. "I'll have Edith check on her tonight. If something's wrong, she'll get to the bottom of it."

"Thank you, sir." As he left the office, he glanced toward the small stone cottage Miss Grant occupied with her cousin Ian Tiffany. At least there, she was safe.

Tilly had refused Edith's request to speak with her after she'd seen Mr. Wilcox leave the clinic. He'd seen the hideous mark, she was sure. If Lucas Kerrington got wind of it, what would he do?

Lucas stared at the knife as if it were a pit viper. He'd never pulled a knife on someone, let alone a woman. His head fell into his hands, and he rubbed his face, trying to remove the memory. The look of terror in her eyes had frightened him, and yet, it gave him a sort of power over her.

Leaning back, he thought of how things had changed. It was a harmless flirtation at first. Winks here, soft words there. She'd even seemed quite pleased with his attentions…until he'd touched her. It had only been a slight touch of her cheek. While she'd pulled away, he'd pursued her, enraptured by the smoothness of her skin. It was like imported rum, and he, an alcoholic.

He stood and threw his hands in the air. He'd never meant to scare her…kiss her, yes, hold her, yes, and see where things went from there. He would never hurt her…

"But she doesn't know that."

The edge of the closed blade glinted in the candlelight, and he scooped it off the coffee table. As long as she feared him, she would obey.

Thomas watched Tilly enter the stone chapel which housed the church of Christ at Harriford Grange with her cousin Ian. They sat down beside Louisa Musgrave, Ian's fiancée. Tilly kept her head down, her neck covered with a white kerchief. He glanced out the door as Mrs. Kerrington entered. Hovering just outside was Lucas Kerrington. Strange. He didn't know he'd moved back to town. He followed the path of Lucas's eyes and landed on Tilly Grant. He looked back to Lucas. The man watched Miss Grant intently before walking out of sight back down the lane. Moving from his usual seat, Thomas went to the Byrnes' pew.

"Doctor."

"Good day, Mr. Wilcox," Colm replied. "How are you on this fine Lord's Day morning?"

"Pardon me, sir, but did Mrs. Byrne have a chance to speak with Miss Grant?"

"Unfortunately, no. Tilly wouldn't see her. It seems she may even be avoiding us. Edith had hoped to speak with her today, but she's been confined to bed rest. Doctor's orders, you know."

Thomas smiled at Dr. Byrne's attempt at humor, but his face quickly sobered.

"Have you noticed anything else, Thomas?"

"Well, it may be nothing, but wasn't Mrs. Byrne helping care for Mrs. Kerrington?"

"Yes, she was. However, Tilly took over a couple of weeks ago."

"That's what I thought."

"What does this have to do with...that matter we discussed?"

"Do you know Lucas Kerrington, Mrs. Kerrington's son?"

"No. I haven't had the pleasure."

Thomas grunted. "A pleasure, Doctor, it would not be."

"Ah. So you think this Lucas Kerrington may be involved?"

As he looked back to Tilly, his heart sank. "I think it's a very strong possibility."

"Miss Grant!"

Tilly's head jerked up at the masculine voice. "Mr. Wilcox. Good morning, sir. How do you do?" He'd caught her just outside the church. Ian was going to luncheon with Louisa while Tilly intended to go straight home. The butcher's warm brown eyes crinkled at the corners when he smiled down at her.

"Fine, miss. How are you doing?" He asked this with real curiosity and waited for her answer.

"I...I'm alright. Yes, I am. I was just heading home. You see, Ian, my cousin, you know, he's engaged to Louisa Musgrave, and she invited him to dine with her, and well, I'm...just going home." She clamped her mouth shut. Why was she rambling like a deranged hen?

Thomas seemed to come to a decision of some sort and bowed his head. Good. He was leaving.

"Miss Grant, would you do me the honor of dining with me at The Tea Biscuit? My treat." He looked so hopeful and so kind, her resolve faltered. He offered her his arm, and together, they walked to the restaurant.

Once inside, they were seated at a table in the back close to the kitchen and sheltered by some potted plants. She ordered a modest meal and waited for him to order. He added a pot of chamomile tea and two orders of molten fudge cake with vanilla ice cream.

"My, Mr. Wilcox, you didn't need to do that!" she exclaimed. Now she would be here all afternoon.

Thomas smiled her way, but when he didn't speak, she looked about the room. A few families from church had come in, but most of the tables were filled with non-churchgoers. She turned back to find him watching her. He blushed and began to rearrange his silverware.

"Miss Grant, you may think it strange, me asking you out like this, but I hoped we might...um...could talk."

A cold hand gripped her chest. He'd seen Lucas' mark. Would he bring it up? He reached over to pat her hand, but she pulled it away. She didn't wish for the touch of any man.

"Mr. Wilcox, I appreciate your kindness, but I have nothing to say to you." She started to get up, but he stood, clasping his hands contritely.

"I'm sorry, Miss Grant. Please sit down."

For some reason, she complied. Their food arrived, and gradually, they began to talk and eventually laugh, all earlier awkwardness fading away. She watched him as he scooped up the last of his ice cream, a little bit of fudge getting on his chin.

"Here, use this," she said, wetting her cloth napkin. As she handed it over to him, their fingers touched, sending an odd little jolt up her arm.

"Thank you," he replied, grinning.

She accepted his offer to walk her home, and they paused on the front porch. They held each other's gaze for a moment before he reached for her hand. She allowed him to take it, forgetting Lucas Kerrington for a moment.

"It was a pleasure spending time with you, Miss Grant. I hope you might consider dining with me again."

"It was, Mr. Wilcox. I would be honored." His smile lit up his handsome face, and she felt her heart warming toward him.

"See you this evening?"

"Yes, of course." She reached for the door knob before turning back. "Would you...would you like to go together this evening? Ian won't be back until after church."

"It would be an honor, Miss Grant." He bowed again, and she was almost sure he was whistling before he was out of sight. What had come over her? Whatever it was, she liked it very much.

Lucas groaned within himself as he hid behind a tree across the street from the small stone cottage. He'd watched them dine together at the tearoom for over two hours. What interest did that big oaf Thomas Wilcox have in Matilda? And what interest did she have in him? True, they were of the same social class, but he'd known Thomas in school, and the butcher was no ladies' man. Lucas had only refrained from mocking him due to how large and muscular he was.

Pulling up past memories, Lucas knew he *was* a ladies' man. Women threw themselves at him, well, all except Matilda. He huffed. Maybe at forty, he was finally losing his touch. He began his walk home pondering why he'd just spent the past two hours doing surveillance on a mere ladies' maid and her oaf of a suitor. In two days, he would be leaving this backwater town. Bernice was coming, and as she was rich and excessively gullible, he fully intended to marry her. As long as Matilda didn't rat on him, he could get off scot-free and leave Thomas Wilcox to pick up the pieces.

Tilly ignored another request from Edith. She'd heard Lucas tell his mother that he would be leaving on Wednesday morning. If she could only hold him off until then, she would be safe. On Monday morning, she set off for Mrs. Kerrington's house, hoping desperately that her son would be out.

She was surprised when Lucas didn't greet her at the door and wasn't in his mother's room. He didn't even appear in the kitchen. She relaxed until sharply at four o'clock when the front door burst open, revealing an extravagantly dressed raven-haired woman, two maids, and a harried Lucas Kerrington. Tilly stepped forward to assist the maids with the luggage before escaping to the kitchen. The maids came in twittering about Lucas until they saw her sitting tensely at the table. She gave them a brief tour before scampering up to Mrs. Kerrington's room.

A man's hand stopped her from turning the knob and pulled her into an alcove. She backed as far as she could against the wall. He didn't come to her. In fact, he seemed distracted.

"Mr. Kerrington?" she asked, not really wanting to offer her assistance.

"She's early."

"Ah."

He covered his forehead with his hand as he peered up and down the hallway. Finding it empty, he stepped closer.

"Look, Mat...Tilly, I know I've been a cad." When she didn't respond, he continued. "You are a beautiful woman, Miss Grant, and well, I find myself very attracted to you." She started to dart away, but he grabbed her arm. "Please hear me out."

The plea in his voice stopped her even as her doubts waged war in her mind. What was he up to?

"I...I would like another chance...to show you I'm not really terrible." He gave a winsome smile, his blue eyes sparkling.

"But you're leaving Wednesday!" she blurted out.

"Maybe," he chuckled. "Unless I have a reason to stay."

Cold chills shot through her. Was it another threat?

"What do you want, Mr. Kerrington?"

"Bernice will be spending tomorrow out with my mother, and I...I was hoping you might grant me the honor of escorting you about the grounds."

"No. I'm sorry, but my answer is no."

"A row on the lake, perhaps?"

He casually pulled out his knife and began to fidget with it. The thought of him using it on her terrified her to the core.

"A row on the lake?" she squeaked.

67

"Just my way of thanking you for taking such good care of Mother."

The blade flickered menacingly. She gulped. "I'd...I'd love to, Mr. Kerrington." He slipped the instrument back into his pocket and reached for her hand.

"Until tomorrow," he said, refraining from his usual kiss. And then, he was gone. A tight knot clinched her chest and stayed there all night long. She would have to be on her guard tomorrow, but it should hold the last of her contact with the horrid Lucas Kerrington.

Thomas looked at the clock. She was late – by half an hour. Tuesday was the day when Tilly arrived early to pick out her meat for the next day, and she never faltered. A sick feeling grew in his gut. He left the shop in his assistant's care and hurried to her cottage. He banged on the door, but no one stirred inside. He ran to the clinic next door and was informed that she'd gone to Mrs. Kerrington's and had not returned home. Running most of the way, Thomas arrived to find the Kerrington house unoccupied. He turned a circle, looking for any explanation of where Tilly might be.

Hearing voices, he followed them toward a large manmade pond. A woman's scream pulled his attention to the right bank, and he rushed toward it. A woman clad in a sopping wet blue gown stumbled onto the shore. An equally drenched man in a tan summer suit lunged toward her and pulled her to him in an effort to kiss her. *Tilly!* Filled with rage, Thomas grabbed Lucas by the collar and punched him, sending the lightweight staggering into the water. He landed with a satisfying *splash!* Tilly fell to the ground, her green eyes wide with shock and her auburn hair cascading down her back in soggy waves.

"Are you alright?" Thomas asked, kneeling by Tilly. She shook violently, even though the day was sweltering. He started to put his arm around her, but she jerked away, and after getting tangled in her skirt a couple of times, she managed to stand. Hiking up her skirt, she ran toward the house. Sighing, Thomas turned to Lucas who was stomping up the bank.

"Was that really necessary?" Lucas asked, rubbing his jaw. "I'm leaving tomorrow."

He'd never understood Lucas. What decent man wouldn't have done the same? Then again, Lucas had never been a decent man.

"How dare you! Miss Grant is a respectable woman, and you were taking advantage of her."

"Hardly. She wouldn't let me."

"You're despicable," Thomas growled. He should haul this cad to the police, but first, he needed to check on Tilly.

"I was only trying to show her how much I appreciated her service to my mother. No harm was done other than our ruined clothes."

"No harm? You assaulted her in broad daylight!"

"I believe you're trespassing."

Thomas drew close to him, overshadowing Lucas' slim frame. The smaller man took note and backed up a step.

"I saw the mark, Lucas. You forced her to be intimate."

"Yes, alright...I kissed her. Don't hit me! Really, I...I didn't force her to...you know, if that's what you're thinking. You can ask her yourself."

The man was insane, but somehow, Thomas believed him. He was the type to brag about his success. He plowed a straight shot back to the house, and upon entering, called for Tilly. She was in the kitchen, huddled by the fire, the gown piled in a dirty heap and her work dress back on her small frame. He wanted to take her in his arms, to tell her she was safe, but as soon as she noticed him, she yelped.

"Stay away from me! For goodness sake, stay away!" Tears streamed down her face and her shoulders shook.

"You're safe, Miss Grant. I won't let him hurt you again. Come. I'll take you home."

She shook her head and darted out the door. He followed her toward town, knowing he could overtake her, but he didn't. He recognized the look in her eyes. She was afraid...of him.

Dr. Byrne was in his front garden when Tilly ran up. He dropped his watering can and met her in the street. Taking her by the shoulders, he forced her to focus on him.

"Tilly! Tilly! What's wrong?"

"Mr. Kerrington! Mr. Wilcox! Fight...so scared..." She couldn't manage a cohesive sentence. Dr. Byrne hushed her and led her into the clinic. Marjorie Robards, the receptionist, got her a drink of water and left her alone with the doctor.

"Take a deep breath, Tilly, and drink some water. There you go. Feel better?" She nodded, her shudders beginning to calm. "Now, tell me, what is all this about?"

"I...I can't say. He threatened me."

"Who threatened you?" She didn't answer. "Did Mr. Kerrington hurt you, Tilly?"

She closed her eyes and felt her tears betraying her.

"I see. I'll call the police."

"No! He has a knife!"

Opening her eyes, she told Dr. Byrne everything, starting with Lucas' arrival and ending with her flight home.

"So you see, Doctor, why I'm so afraid."

"I wish you'd have told Edith about his behavior. We could have found someone to take your place. He should be punished. Please allow me to call the constable."

"Alright."

Dr. Byrne sent Tilly upstairs to the guest room while he called the constable and talked to his wife. Edith was distraught and sent for Tilly immediately. Tilly related to her friend other matters as well, those of her heart.

Lucas Kerrington was released on bail the next day and left town with his fiancée, his tail between his legs. Thomas had given his statement, half expecting to be charged himself. He felt he'd somehow done wrong, at least in the eyes of Miss Grant. She refused to see him, so he kept his distance.

"She'll come around," said Mr. Stevens, the elderly preacher. "You'll see. She's been through a terrible ordeal, and she needs time to process her feelings."

"I know," Thomas replied. "I may have overreacted, punching him. She seemed even more afraid of me than him."

"Son, you were protecting her. You did the right thing. Miss Grant knows this, but it may take time for her to accept that you're not like Mr. Kerrington, that you won't use your strength against her."

"I would never hurt her! I...I love her!" he exclaimed, pain accompanying those three simple words. He hadn't known how strong his attachment was until he'd seen Lucas holding her. "What if she never wants anything to do with me?"

"Give her time, Thomas. Mrs. Byrne will let you know when she thinks Miss Grant is willing to see you. Until then, spend time in prayer and the scriptures. In God's word are all of the answers you seek. You are a righteous man. Show her that you love God as well as her, and you will win back her heart."

"Win *back* her heart?" Thomas asked, confused. Mr. Stevens winked his eye. Could Tilly have loved him in return?

Tilly sat serenely by the open window in Edith's bedroom. A week had passed since the ordeal, and she felt quite recovered physically. However, her heart's wounds were not so quick to heal.

"I should have come to you," she said, looking down at her rough, work-worn hands. "I was so afraid of him, though."

"I know, my dear," replied Edith soothingly. "In times such as those, we're all bound to suffer from poor judgment. At least, thanks to the good Lord, you were not hurt by him, in body that is."

Tilly brushed away a tear. "At first, I was flattered that such a handsome man noticed me. I hoped that one day he might really care for me. How foolish!"

Edith allowed Tilly time to reflect in silence. Her heart swelled with love for her dear friend and part-time employer.

"Has Mr. Wilcox called recently?" Tilly asked in feigned disinterest. Edith's smile was sympathetic.

"No. Not so far as I've been told."

"What must he think of me, Edith, wearing that awful dress and being...by that odious man?" She couldn't bring herself to say it. "And how I screamed at him! He, a knight coming to my rescue, and I...all I did was fear him. He's probably happy to be rid of me!"

"Nonsense, Tilly! Mr. Wilcox knows you were not to blame."

"But I was, Edith. Don't you see? I went along with his scheme..."

"Because you were afraid he'd hurt you! Really, Tilly, don't give that notion another thought!"

"I feel like a broken pitcher or a dirty handkerchief. Used and then discarded. He deserves someone fresh and innocent."

"Tilly, dear, come sit by me." Tilly sat on the edge of the bed and took Edith's offered hand. Edith wiped a stray auburn hair from her face. "You are not broken or dirty. You were washed in the blood of Jesus, and the Father has forgiven you of any sin you may have committed in the business with Mr. Kerrington. Mr. Wilcox thinks no less of you. In fact, I believe he is very much in love."

Doubt still held firm in her mind as she pondered Edith's words. "Why hasn't he come?"

"Are you ready to see him?"

"I am," Tilly replied. "I long to see him and to see for myself how he feels...if he could ever love me again."

For some awful reason, Thomas couldn't get the image of that dress out of his mind. It had been more elegant and more expensive than anything she had ever worn. Who had given it to her? It had to have been Lucas, but more importantly, why had she agreed to wear it?

Lucas Kerrington had always been a favorite with the ladies. His trim physique and northern looks earned him many long glances and walking companions. On the contrary, Thomas' Sally had been the only woman ever interested in him. He wasn't such a bad-looking fellow, and his job kept him in good physical shape, but he'd never been compared favorably to Lucas. It was highly possible that Miss Grant had been one of the many women who'd been snared in his trap.

And then there was the matter of her rejection. He'd gone to find her, to rescue her if need be, and she'd fled from him. That stung more than he cared to admit.

The bell over the shop door rang, bringing him out of his reverie. He stayed in the back room, allowing his assistant to wait on the customer.

"Pardon me, sir, but is Mr. Wilcox in?" asked a light feminine voice. He moved over to the door and peeked out. Miss Grant stood mere feet from him, looking radiant in a plain green calico work dress, her auburn hair arranged becomingly beneath her straw hat.

"He's busy at the moment, ma'am. I'll tell him you called." The boy was doing exactly as he'd told him, but why didn't he rush out there? She wanted to speak to him...but why?

"Thank you." Her countenance dimmed, and she turned to leave.

"Wait! Miss Grant, please wait!" he called, yanking off his apron and washing his hands and arms. She stood patiently for him, and he escorted her outside. "Did you wish to see me?"

"Yes, Mr. Wilcox, I did. I...I wanted to thank you for coming to my rescue the other day and for your kindness and concern for my welfare. If not for you, I don't know what might have happened."

Thomas only nodded, his characteristic shyness returning. She was subdued. Lucas' actions had doused her fiery spirit, and he was at a loss how to ignite those embers once again.

"Edith has found someone else to care for Mrs. Kerrington," she explained softly. "The poor lady is beside herself with worry. She sent three dozen roses by way of making amends. I never held her to blame."

When Thomas still didn't respond, she bid him good day. He watched her lovely figure until it was out of sight, feeling for all the world like a fool.

He hated her. It was the only explanation. Any love he'd harbored for her had long sailed away just as she was beginning to understand her own heart. Her love, once small and tender, had grown into a mighty cedar, prepared to build the halls of Solomon's palace, but now, Mr. Wilcox deemed it only good for firewood. She prayed every day that his thoughts might return to her.

Days turned into weeks as she slipped back into her routine. Every evening, she stopped by the butcher shop, and every evening, she returned home with only his meat to satisfy her. Cousin Ian, concerned for her welfare, urged her to try once more to share her heart with Mr. Wilcox, his own romance blinding him to the non-existence of hers. In a few short weeks, Ian would wed Louisa and move into the fine home the Musgraves had given the couple. Moving up from farrier, he was now manager of the entire Rosewood Stud. God had infinitely blessed her cousin, and she was more than pleased for him.

One evening as she was entering the butcher shop, she noticed a new figure standing behind the counter in Mr. Wilcox's customary spot. Momentarily disoriented, she halted and looked about. Standing off to the side, a tall, well-built gentleman held a bouquet of dahlias toward her. Dressed in his best suit, the handsome brown-eyed butcher bowed and offered her his arm.

"Miss Grant, would you do me the honor of accompanying me on a walk?" They shared a mutual blush at the whistles which emanated from behind the counter. She reached for his arm, and he pulled her gently to his side.

"I would be honored, Mr. Wilcox," she said, smiling up at him. Those sweet little crinkles enhanced his smile and sent butterflies to her heart.

Thomas led her down the lane past The Tea Biscuit to a quiet grove. The evening light filtered through the trees, and the cheerful birds sang a song meant only for them. They sat together on a wooden bench, enjoying the peaceful atmosphere.

"Miss Grant?"

"Yes, Mr. Wilcox?"

"I've been praying for you these past few weeks. In fact, you're always in my thoughts."

"Am I?" she asked, appearing rather breathless. "And are these recollections good or bad?"

"Good. Most definitely good."

"You're often in my thoughts as well." He grinned at this and dared to place his arm around her. She snuggled into his side, and he squeezed her shoulder. How perfectly she fit by him! He slid his finger down her pale cheek, pleased that she didn't flinch.

"Miss Grant, I know I'm only an old widower, and my job is, well, what it is..."

She held her tiny finger up to his lips. "You're not old, and I don't care what you do."

"I could provide a good home for you. It wouldn't be anything fancy, but it would be comfortable and safe."

"I'm not worried about riches, Mr. Wilcox." Her shamrock eyes looked earnestly into his, and he debated kissing her. He cleared his throat instead. All of her past reserve seemed to have faded. He could sense her unspoken love, but what he needed above all else was to hear it without feeling he'd prompted her. He glanced out at the trees, at the birds, and then, back at Tilly.

"Miss Grant..."

"Tilly," she corrected, covering his cheek with her hand. She tipped her chin up, and he fought his growing urge. This conversation had gone much more smoothly in his head.

"I'm sorry, Tilly. I'm not very good at this sort of thing."

She giggled – a musical, tinkling sound.

"I can see that, Thomas," she replied, caressing his jaw. "It's alright. I love you, you know."

"You do?"

"I do."

He grinned from ear to ear until she sat back in consternation.

"Well?" she huffed. "Do you love me?"

"I do...very, very much," he replied before pulling her in for that much wanted kiss.

The doubt and anxiety brought into their lives by one Lucas Kerrington was all forgotten as they shared their love and planned for the future. Although the ordeal left its scars, time and prayer healed the wounds and allowed love to blossom once again. Thomas sighed contentedly as he held Tilly in the fading light. God was good, indeed.

The Shopkeeper's Love

Lucas Kerrington felt like a cad. Oh, he knew he'd been one for most of his life, but he'd never *felt* like one before. After leaving Harriford Grange with Bernice Ralston, his former fiancée, he had been informed by her father that their engagement was off. No daughter of his would marry a convict. Lucas had protested that it had all been a misunderstanding and would soon be put to rights, but the only response he'd received was an ornately-carved teak door in his face. When Miss Tilly Grant had decided to press charges, Lucas had been shuffled from jail to courtroom, given a five-year sentence, and taken to prison. It had all happened so quickly, he'd barely had any time to process the events.

Once incarcerated, Lucas learned the true meaning of fear. Never a violent man, he'd tried to stay out of sight and mind of his fellow prisoners. He had been the victim of a much blown-up scandal, and he had no real reason to be there. But there, he was. Unfortunately, the big guys were fully aware of that fact. He'd longed for a slug from Thomas Wilcox in place of the beatings he received in prison.

Soon after entering the "big house," as his fellow inmates called it, he'd been invited to do a Bible study with one of the local preachers. He'd scoffed at the idea. What use had he for God? He would do his time, and if he survived, he would leave the place and go somewhere far, far away. Preferably somewhere with beautiful women and very little responsibility.

It's funny how three years in a place like that can change a man. Out of the sheer desire to keep on living, he'd toughened up and learned to stand up for himself. Working long hours of hard labor, he'd developed a muscular frame and calloused hands. At forty-three, he'd also found an emptiness which he couldn't fill. One of his – dare he say *friends* – had been converted only two months before and had talked non-stop about Jesus and the cross and how he'd been saved from his sins. Cautiously intrigued, Lucas agreed to a study, just one, to see what it was all about.

The preacher, a Mr. Sanderson, used his well-worn Bible to show Lucas Jesus' path to the cross and His resurrection. He talked of God's love for him and took him to a passage about a man named Saul. Saul had effectively been a mass murderer, hauling Christians off to jail simply because he misunderstood their faith and the reason for their hope. One day as Saul was seeking more devout souls, Jesus appeared to him. He asked Saul why he was fighting against God, which was a losing battle indeed. Saul was made blind for three days in which he prayed fervently for forgiveness. In that time, he realized he needed to learn more about Jesus. In His infinite knowledge, Jesus had sent a Christian by the name of Ananias to teach Saul the gospel and show him how he might be saved from his sins. He said that baptism would wash away his sins, thus allowing him to call on the name of the Lord.

This tale had eaten at Lucas. He didn't sleep much in the week afterward, searching the scriptures with Mr. Sanderson's notes in hand which showed him how his former lifestyle had been so very wrong. He'd been guilty of greed, covetousness, and fornication, among other things. If God could save a man like Saul, was it possible He could save Lucas as well?

By the day of the next study, Lucas was ready to become a Christian. Mr. Sanderson explained to him how his life must change to reflect Christ and how he must continue to study and grow in the knowledge of the gospel. Lucas understood this and confessed his conviction that Jesus was indeed the Christ, the Son of God. He'd repented mournfully for his past sins and wished for nothing more than to have them washed away. The water of the baptistery was as cold as ice as Lucas stepped into it with Mr. Sanderson. He allowed himself to be lowered down, immersed completely. The sense of relief which greeted him upon being raised was so great, it brought tears to his eyes. He exclaimed praises to God, hugged Mr. Sanderson tightly, and with much inner peace, allowed himself to be returned to his cell.

He'd seen the preacher many times over the past two years as he came to lead worship services for the inmates. Elders from the local congregation along with a few male members had taken turns teaching him and praying with him. He'd taken great comfort in the thought that their congregation prayed for him by name at every service. Lucas worked hard on his own prayer life and his studies. While some of his fellow inmates had mocked him viciously, several had studied with him and had also been converted. As he reflected on his life, he thanked God for the blessing his incarceration had become.

The train pulled to a smooth stop at the station, and Lucas, waking from his reverie, collected his things and exited onto the platform. As he went in search of a cab, he wondered not for the first time what the citizens of Harriford Grange would think of his arrival.

Tilly Wilcox looked at the man across from her with reservations. Lucas Kerrington had caused her more grief than anyone she'd ever known. He'd caressed her, kissed her, and would have tried to have his way with her if her beloved Thomas hadn't come to her rescue. She shuddered involuntarily at the thought. When her husband had proposed this meeting, she'd put her foot down. She had no desire to set her eyes upon her attacker. However, as she sat at a table in Mr. Stevens' office with Thomas beside her, all she felt was pity. Time had not been good to Lucas. His blond hair was now mostly gray, and his blue eyes were dull. Although he'd gained muscularity in prison, his body appeared worn and haggard. Ghastly scars littered his face and hands, making her think of a pirate.

The location of the meeting had been agreed upon by all parties, including Constable Craig MacKinnon who stood just out of earshot in case things went poorly. Thomas patted her hand and motioned to Lucas.

"Miss...*Mrs.* Wilcox," Lucas began, "thank you for agreeing to meet with me. I know this must be very difficult for you." Tilly nodded. Lucas cleared his throat and continued. "I wish to apologize for my actions toward you. I was very wrong to take advantage of you, and I assure you, it will not happen again." He proceeded to tell them briefly the story of his conversion and the changes he was making in his life. "As you know, my mother left me her estate when she passed last year. It is my desire to make the necessary repairs and settle there. However, if my presence in Harriford Grange makes you uncomfortable," he waved his hand to include both her and her husband, "then I will leave immediately and sell the property through my solicitor."

Tilly looked down at Thomas' large hand covering hers. How would she feel with the possibility of seeing Lucas at any time? Her husband was not always with her, and she often took her two children out alone. She smiled as she thought of her boy and girl. Frank was older and red-haired like his mother, while little Harriet had the brown hair of her father. Both shared an unusual set of hazel eyes which made her mother's heart burst with love. What would she do if she met Lucas alone?

"Please stay, Mr. Kerrington," she found herself saying. "If what you say about your conversion is true, and you are truly sorry for your actions toward me, it would be unfair for me to turn you out of your home."

"All of it is true, I assure you, Mrs. Wilcox," Lucas replied earnestly. "It is my wish to start over here and live the rest of my life in service to the Lord. I can promise you I have no other intentions."

"Well then," said Thomas, looking to his wife for confirmation, "I believe this meeting is concluded." He held his hand out to Lucas who hesitated only a moment before shaking it.

"Do I take this to mean you forgive me, Mrs. Wilcox?" Lucas asked.

"I do, Mr. Kerrington. I'll not say we are friends, but I believe you and hope all goes well for you."

"Would it be alright with you if I began worshiping here?"

Tilly swallowed and looked at her husband. He put his arm around her. "Yes, I think that would be fine. Good day, Mr. Kerrington." He bowed as Thomas escorted her from the room. It would take some getting used to, but she hoped that over time, God would help her to fully trust Lucas Kerrington.

Lucas busied himself making notes on the much needed repairs of the Kerrington family home. His mother had been too ill to see to them, and he had been too lazy to do his part. No more, he thought. If he put his back to the work, he would soon have a comfortable home and an improved reputation.

His thoughts drifted back to the meeting that morning. Mrs. Wilcox was even more beautiful than before, her loving marriage the most likely cause. If only he'd played his cards right...no, she'd deserved much better than the man he was then. Thomas Wilcox was indeed a very lucky and blessed man. He asked God's forgiveness for his thoughts and for the strength to be a better man. He'd determined before leaving prison that he would remain single and live out his days in service to God. No woman should have to put up with a past like his, even though it had been forgiven. He made a few measurements, stuck his flat cap on his head, and headed off to town.

Anne Freiburg watched the stranger with open interest. Tall and big-boned, she'd never been cursed with the vanity which robbed other women of their innocence. She smiled brightly as he approached the counter.

"Good morning, sir! Velcome to Freiburg's Hardware and Sundries. How can I help you?"

He avoided eye contact as he scanned a piece of paper, his straight grey-blonde hair drawing her attention. Forty-five to fifty, she guessed, also noting his height at around her own five-foot-eleven. He was in good shape for his age, but when he raised his head, she held back a gasp. Scars lined his face like spider webs. He must have caught her reaction as he quickly turned away and pointed out into the store.

"I'll just have a look for myself. I'm sure I can find everything."

Contrite, she hurried around the counter. "Please, sir, I'm most villing to help you find vatever it is you need. It vill be much faster, and you'll be on your vay in no time at all." This last part sounded awful, and she started to apologize, but he held up his equally scarred hand.

"Really, miss, I'll be alright on my own...unless you would rather me go elsewhere." He said this with such humility that she felt heat rush to her face.

"May ve start over?" she asked, holding out her hand. "My name is Anne Freiburg, and my parents opened this store four years ago. They've since moved to be closer to my brother Rolfe, so now I run it. I vould be delighted to assist you in any vay. Please allow me."

He smiled shyly as he shook her hand and gave her his list. It took her a mere ten minutes to gather all of the items, except for two which she would have to order. She pulled out her receipt pad and inquired for his name.

"Did I not say it?" he asked.

"No, sir. I don't believe you did."

"I'm very sorry. It's Kerrington, Lucas Kerrington."

The name rang a bell in Anne's mind, but for the life of her, she couldn't remember why. She added up his total, bagged his goods, and sent him on his way, happy that she'd successfully served another customer in her fine shop.

Lucas berated himself as he left the shop. In his former life, he would have scoffed at the solidly-built young woman. With her strawberry-blonde hair and wide jaw, she reminded him of a Viking, albeit a very fine-looking one. It hadn't helped the image that she'd had her hair braided in two buns on the sides of her head and wore an old-fashioned ribbon-laced bodice which had defined her waistline becomingly. What was her name again? Freiburg, that was it. German - which explained the slight accent.

He took a wrong turn on his walk home as he remembered each detail he'd noticed about her. He chided himself and pushed her from his mind. He'd made a commitment not to look at another woman, and he intended to keep it.

Once home, he started to work on his first project. The front porch was sagging, and the door was in serious need of a new coat of paint. He'd decided to start there because, as he saw it, the porch was the focal point of the façade. It either attracted or repelled visitors. Since he was determined to start afresh, he wanted his home to feel welcoming and attractive. He got out his tools and went to work.

A few days later as he dipped his brush into a bucket of coal black paint, Lucas heard the sound of a horse clopping up his drive. He turned from his partially painted front door and took in the sight. The driver, a woman by the looks of it, was guiding a stocky Belgian pulling a wagon. Dumbfounded, he waited until she'd pulled up in front of his newly-repaired porch before speaking.

"May I help you?" he asked.

"Good evening, Mr. Kerrington," said a lightly accented voice. "I brought the rest of your order."

He dropped his brush into the bucket and hurried to help her from her seat. "Miss Freiburg. Did I miss your note? I wasn't aware my goods had arrived."

She adjusted her shawl against the autumn chill and shook her head. "No, sir. Your order arrived after luncheon, and since I knew you vere in great need of it, I decided to bring it by on my vay home."

"I would have gladly waited until morning, Miss Freiburg." She appeared a trifle hurt by this, so he changed his tone. "It was very kind of you to think of me. I'll unload everything so you can be on your way."

She assisted him in unloading his cargo, even though he protested strongly. "Mr. Kerrington, I may be a lady, but I'm not a veakling. It is my duty to see that each of my customers is satisfied vith my service."

She'd lost her shawl before their unloading and unconsciously reached up to undo the top button of her blouse. His eyes followed her hand, and he caught a glimpse of the hollow of her throat before he forced his gaze away.

"Vould it be too forward to ask for a glass of vater, Mr. Kerrington?" she asked innocently. He needed to hurry her along or his thoughts wouldn't be so innocent.

"Of course, Miss Freiburg. I'll be back in a moment." He rushed inside and splashed water on his face. *Lord, is this some sort of test, this woman coming here? Please give me the strength to see her off!* Feeling fortified, he got her a glass of cool water from the handy pump in the kitchen.

Mr. Kerrington's behavior was certainly peculiar, Anne pondered. Most men treated her with respect as if she were their little sister or perhaps a cousin. This stranger, however, seemed rattled around her, and this puzzled her exceedingly.

Even at thirty-years-old, Anne had never had a suitor – unless one counted Hans who gave her a flower when she was eleven, and that had been done on a dare. Men didn't seem to find her as attractive as the petite *frauleins*, but she'd made peace with that long ago. She had her store and a town and church full of good friends. She was happy.

Lucas entered the stone chapel and headed for the back. Perhaps no one would recognize him until he'd established himself as a member in good standing.

"Mr. Kerrington!" called a now familiar voice. "Mr. Kerrington!"

No such luck. Miss Anne Freiburg was waving dramatically to him from near the podium as the rest of the congregation fell into a hushed stare. To make matters worse, she was standing next to Mrs. Wilcox who looked like she would rather fall through the floor than see him. He caught her eye, silently requesting permission to approach. She nodded briefly and turned to care for one of her children. Lucas drew near Miss Freiburg and bowed humbly, thankful that most of the members had resumed their activities.

"Oh, Mr. Kerrington! I'm so delighted to see you here. Are you a member of the church?" she asked, her amber eyes sparkling bright. He'd noticed their golden color as well as their almond shape days ago but hadn't allowed himself to contemplate them.

"I am. I see you are as well?"

"I am. Mrs. Vilcox, my friend here, she taught me the gospel ven ve first moved here. I vas so eager to learn vat made her so happy. Now I am happy too, except I don't have a husband!" She said the last part with a giggle, but he detected wistfulness in her words.

"I'm surprised," he heard himself say. Mrs. Wilcox jerked around and stared warning darts at him over Anne's shoulder. Miss Freiburg only laughed.

"That's too kind of you, Mr. Kerrington. Oh, vill you sit vith us? There's plenty of room."

Thomas had joined them at this point, and Lucas, feeling he'd long overstayed his welcome, started to make his excuses.

"Nonsense," called the butcher. "You're more than welcome to sit with us." Tilly quietly agreed, and he found himself sitting on the end of the pew trying his best not to touch Miss Freiburg's pink satin skirt. She leaned conspiratorially toward him, making his efforts futile.

"Mr. Kerrington, I do hope you'll join us for luncheon at The Tea Biscuit. It vould be a shame for you to miss Miss Isabelle's cream scones with lemon curd." She pursed her shapely coral lips as he considered what he'd gotten himself into. She had no idea how gorgeous she was, making ignoring her impossible.

"I would be delighted, Miss Freiburg, provided your friends approve."

"Of course they approve, Mr. Kerrington," she said, batting her red-gold eyelashes. "Class is about to start, but I'm so excited!"

He stared at her a moment longer before being drawn to Mrs. Wilcox's stern gaze. He smiled kindly and turned his focus to the lesson.

Anne couldn't understand her friend's consternation. "But he's been forgiven, Tilly."

"Yes, Anne. He's repented and been forgiven."

"Then shouldn't *ve* forgive him and give him another chance?"

Tilly thought about this before laying her hand on Anne's arm. They were in the vestibule during the break between the class and service. "It's not that I haven't forgiven him, Anne, but I can't stand by and watch my best friend be ogled by the man who almost ruined me."

"He vasn't ogling me!"

"Alright – *staring*. He *was* staring at you."

Anne blushed. "I don't see vhy. I'm not beautiful like you or Louisa or Mrs. Byrne."

Tilly rubbed her arm affectionately. "Dearest Anne, you are *too* beautiful for your own good. You're simply too humble to see it. I'm not at all surprised he noticed. However..."

"No man's ever thought me beautiful. I'm not about to start imagining such things now. He is a good Christian man, and I vant to make him feel velcome."

"Alright, Anne, but if he makes one false move, you had best come straight to me."

"Your vorry is in vain, my friend, but I promise you I vill," Anne agreed with a sigh. She had no qualms about Mr. Kerrington, but she would keep her friend's advice in mind.

Lucas thoroughly enjoyed Anne's company at luncheon, but he didn't let his guard down for a minute. He'd heard Tilly say, probably for his ears, that Anne was fifteen years his junior. He wondered why she wasn't married and chalked it up to the poor taste of his fellow man. He'd not risked an offer to walk her home and was currently perched on a ladder attempting to remove one of his broken shutters. He'd decided to do as much on the outside of the house as he could before the cold set in. Then, he would turn his attention to the inside.

He was excited about this project. It made him feel useful and industrious - two words which failed to describe his first forty-three years. He was making this house his home, and a fine home it would be. With only minor re-pointing, the red brick two-story with its perfectly symmetrical face would be a beacon to the community, heralding the power of second chances.

He laid the shutter on top of two saw horses and began to strip off layers of chipped paint. As he pondered whether to paint them black like the door, the lovely amber of Miss Freiburg's eyes popped into his mind. Would he dare? He forced himself to move the black paint close by and get back to work.

Anne made extra preparations to her appearance each morning, secretly hoping Mr. Kerrington would stop by. Being a young Christian herself, she knew what it was like to struggle with one's past. She hoped that maybe their friendship would be as much of an encouragement to him as it was to her.

She was rewarded one quiet afternoon when Mr. Kerrington came in to buy some more nails. She watched him as he approached the counter and blushed a little at the appreciation in his eyes.

"Good afternoon, Mr. Kerrington," she enthused. "Vat can I get for you today?"

It took him a good minute to find his words, and she blushed more deeply when he did. "Would you go to dinner with me this evening, Miss Freiburg?" Her mouth formed an 'O,' and he backtracked. "Perhaps not, after all. Your friends would not be accompanying us."

"On the contrary, Mr. Kerrington, I vould love to dine vith you. I close the shop at five o'clock. Vould you like to drop by then?"

He went as still as a marble statue. Perhaps he regretted his invitation already. "Five...five o'clock? Yes, that's perfect."

"If you'd rather not..." she replied, feeling a bit like a spoiled child.

"No, I would rather go...with you." This made her smile brightly.

"Five o'clock then, Mr. Kerrington. Don't be late!"

A wonderful grin lit up his scarred face before he remembered why he was in the store in the first place. Anne's belly fluttered as she gathered up his order and sent him on his way.

What had possessed him to ask Miss Freiburg to dinner? Her hair, he decided. She'd done it up in curls all over the crown of her head, reminding him of a duchess. The sweet glow of her cheeks had sealed the deal. He made himself focus on putting up his freshly painted black shutters. It was only dinner...as friends, nothing more. Afterwards, he would walk her to her door – if she wanted him to – and then, he would be on his way. She was a lady, and he was determined to leave her exactly that.

When he arrived at exactly five o'clock, it appeared business had been rather slow that afternoon. Miss Freiburg's curls were slightly rearranged, a few dangling tantalizingly by her ears, and she'd changed into a different dress. This one, while modestly covering her feminine curves, showed off her figure to full advantage. The sage bodice and full cream skirt added to his earlier picture of a duchess. She was radiant as he shyly offered her his arm. Not for the first time, he wondered what he'd gotten himself into.

Anne ignored the curious glances they received as they walked to dinner. Instead of The Tea Biscuit, he'd chosen the nicer Heritage Inn Restaurant. Her heart beat wildly as she wondered if this might be her first real date. After the host saw them to their table, Lucas pulled out her chair and seated himself across from her. They placed their orders and settled down to wait.

"You look lovely this evening," Lucas said, smiling kindly. "Have you been to this restaurant before?"

"*Danke*. I mean, thank you," she replied, her face heating up. "I have only been once, ven my parents vere living here. It's a very good restaurant. I'm happy to return."

"I'm happy to be the one to bring you here," he replied jovially. His manner toward her, although very gentlemanly, was not terribly romantic. Perhaps it wasn't a date after all. She sobered a little, but she was determined to enjoy herself no matter what it was called.

"Have you made much progress on your home?" she asked. "I vould love to see it again."

He choked on his water, and after coughing a moment, began to tell her what changes he'd made.

"I vould *love* to see it again."

"Perhaps sometime," he replied noncommittally.

The arrival of their food saved them both from the uncomfortable moment. As they tucked in to the delicious fare, their conversation warmed, and soon they were both laughing as she told him of her youth on a farm on the continent.

"So you named the pig after your father? What did he say to that?" Lucas asked.

"He said it was a *gut* thing it hadn't been a cow!" Tears streamed down their faces, and at that moment, she knew she would enjoy spending even more time with Mr. Kerrington.

The dreaded moment arrived as they left the restaurant.

"Would you like me to walk you home?" he asked, half hoping she would say *no*. Her smile was slow and shy.

"If you vish to, I would be delighted. It's not far."

She led him off the main lane to a side street lined with modest cottages. She stopped before a neat cream one with lavender lining the walkway. He walked her to the door, and she smiled uncertainly.

"Thank you again, Mr. Kerrington. I had a vonderful time."

He bowed and took a step back. "As did I, Miss..."

"You may call me *Anne*, if you like," she interrupted hopefully. He wanted nothing more...well, almost nothing more than to do so and to hear her say his name in return, but he felt formality would aide him much better.

"Miss Freiburg, I don't believe we should be informal so soon in our acquaintance. Your friends might not approve."

"Perhaps you're right," she replied thoughtfully. "I had so hoped to call you *Lucas*." She threw her pretty hand over her mouth. "Please forgive me, sir! The thought just slipped out!"

She looked so adorable that he had to back up another step. "It's quite alright," he replied. "I should be going."

"Do you vant to come inside for a minute? I have tea, or coffee if you prefer."

He wavered for only an instant before a horrible thought struck him. Knowing his past, God would not approve of him spending any time alone with this woman. She was so innocent and perfect, and if he so much as kissed her once, he would be unable to stop himself. He tugged uncomfortably on his collar.

"I think it's best if I said goodnight now, Miss Freiburg. I had a wonderful time with you this evening."

"Vell, if you must go," she replied sullenly. Then, she took two quick steps toward him and kissed him on the cheek. "Shall I see you again soon?"

He was halfway down the walk before he turned back to wave. "Yes, soon. Very soon. Good night, Miss Freiburg!"

He didn't slow down until he reached his own drive. As his hand went to his cheek, he melted into a glorious puddle before freezing in place. She fancied him! That beautiful creature fancied him, but he'd made a promise not to touch her or any woman. *Heavenly Father,* he prayed, *what am I to do? I know I said I wouldn't seek after a woman, but is it possible You sent her to me? Please help me to see what Your will is in my life and help me to be content with it. Amen.*

"You kissed him?" Tilly exclaimed, pulling little Frank back to her side. "After what I told you?"

"On the cheek," Anne replied, still slightly miffed by his quick departure. She straightened a display of fall gardening tools and looked contentedly around her shop. "I'm not afraid of him."

"Oh, Anne, you are too good! Can you not see the harm this intimacy might bring? What of his past?"

"Talk no more of his past!" Anne exclaimed, rushing past Tilly to scoop up little Harriet. The baby's soft curls tickled her face, calming her frayed emotions a bit.

"Anne, listen to me. His past is forgiven, but that doesn't mean you should drop your guard. And think of him! If he truly wishes to change his ways, your throwing yourself at him is not going to be helpful."

"I didn't think of that. But I vasn't throwing myself at him. I vill keep vat you say in mind. I don't vant to be a stumbling block to him."

Tilly was mostly appeased by her answer, and Anne bid her good day with a sad heart. She had only meant to encourage Lucas. Could her enthusiasm have actually hindered him in his Christian walk?

Against his desires, Lucas waited until he'd used his last nail before he returned to the hardware store. He hoped that the absence would help him put his priorities in line. When he entered the store, the bell tinkling a welcome, he heard Anne's sweet voice call out a greeting. He found her perched atop a ladder in the back of the shop, rearranging some boxes on an upper shelf.

"Oh. Hello, Mr. Kerrington," she said without her usual warmth. She descended the ladder, refusing to make eye contact. "Vat can I help you vith today?"

"Are...are you alright, Miss Freiburg?"

"I suppose." She brushed past him, heading quickly to the counter. She whipped out her receipt book and tapped her pen impatiently. "Vat do you need, Mr. Kerrington?"

She fetched the items on his list with military precision and no small talk. What had brought about this change in her demeanor? Was she upset about their outing? Had he let her down in some way? He dared to reach out and touch her hand. She jumped as if a snake had bitten her.

"Is this all, Mr. Kerrington?"

"Are you sure you're alright? Did I do something to upset you?" At this, her eyes shot up, and she thought long and hard about her response.

"Is this everything you need, sir?"

"Yes," he replied, hurt by her rejection. "I believe so."

She totaled him out and took his money with a quiet *danke* before heading back to her ladder. He left the store with a heavy bag and an even heavier heart.

"What did you do to him?" Tilly whispered during the Wednesday evening announcements. Lucas had opted to sit with another family, and Anne sorely missed his presence.

"I stopped throwing myself at him," she replied a bit more vehemently than she intended. All she'd meant to do was be less enthusiastic, but the effort it had taken to curb her bubbly nature had instead made her cranky toward him. She felt awful but was at a loss as to what to do.

"Do you think you went too far?" When Anne didn't respond, Tilly patted her hand. "If you need to talk, you know I'm always here for you."

Anne shifted just enough to catch a glimpse of Lucas. He was looking at her, but as soon as their eyes met, he turned away. The pained expression on his face stung. Could she find a middle ground between the two extremes of her temper before she lost his friendship forever?

That night, Anne spent a long time in prayer. She wanted to be a good example and friend to Lucas, and she hoped, although cautiously, that he might come to see her in a romantic way. She'd felt a spark with him, and she believed he felt it too. *Dear Lord, please help me to be the voman you vant me to be and a friend to Mr. Kerrington. He is very dear to me, and if it be your vill, of course, I pray he might come to love me as vell. Help me to be patient, and if you don't intend him for me, please help me to be content vith your vill. Amen.*

She was refreshed after her time with the Lord. His will was best after all, even if she didn't like it at the time. She was sure that she would look back on this epoch of her life with satisfaction that God's will had prevailed.

Lucas reminded himself of his prayers for strength as well as self-control, especially when around Anne Freiburg. He smoothed his gray-blonde hair and examined the bouquet in his hand. He'd chosen an autumn blend of red, orange, and yellow. He hoped it would break the ice between them and help him get to the bottom of her strange behavior.

He approached the counter with the flowers behind his back. She was facing away from him, and he noted that she was wearing her hair in a braid around her crown. Woven in were some orange ribbon and small yellow flowers. She shouldn't be working in such a dreary place, he mused. She would be much more suited for a flower shop. Hearing his footfalls, she spun around and clasped her heart.

"Mr. Kerrington! I didn't hear you come in."

"I entered at the same time as Mr. Stevens exited. You seemed too lost in thought to notice."

She quirked an eyebrow at the flowers poking out from behind him. "Vat have you got vith you?" Her smile almost reached her eyes as he displayed the bouquet before her. "It's lovely. Vho is it for?"

"You, of course, Miss Freiburg."

"For me?" she replied with a delighted giggle. She grabbed the blooms and ran to the back room. Returning with a vase, she set his present in full view of all who entered. "*Danke*, Mr. Kerrington! I don't know vat else to say!"

"Say you'll have dinner with me."

Her amber eyes grew as round as saucers. "Tonight?"

"If you're free."

She shook her head. "I'm sorry, Mr. Kerrington. I have a ladies' meeting tonight."

"Tomorrow then?"

She touched her chin and looked up at the ceiling. *"Ja,* I'm free tomorrow."

"I'll pick you up at five?" Her grin lit up her face and fueled the glow in his heart. It seemed that whatever had been bothering her had nothing to do with him after all.

On the way to pick up Miss Freiburg, Lucas mulled over his afternoon. He'd been to talk to Mr. Stevens and one of the elders, a Mr. Bailey, about his concerns regarding a romance with Anne. Since they already knew his past and his recent conversion, he'd proceeded to tell them of his feelings for her and what he hoped she felt for him. They waved off his previous commitment to remain single, stating that God had never intended for man to be alone. Since there were no obstacles to the match, they felt he would do well to pursue her as long as she continued to return his regard.

To this, he'd replied with his apprehension that a long courtship would place undue stress on him. However, he didn't want to pressure her into marriage sooner than she might like. The two men had suggested a very public courtship, meaning always staying within view of at least one other person. This would aide Lucas on the straight and narrow and allow both of them as much time as needed to make an informed decision. It was a sound plan, and he felt bolstered by their prayers for him.

When he arrived at the hardware store, he wondered if she'd heard his thoughts about opening a flower shop. The counter was covered with bouquets of various sizes and colors. While his was most prominently displayed, its beauty was vastly overshadowed by the array.

He stood back and observed her as she finished up with the customers in front of him – two men about her age. The taller one was leaning toward her, whispering something which caused her cheeks to turn a soft pink. The shorter one held up his own rather dismal bouquet of wildflowers, hoping to catch her attention. She smiled sweetly to both men and thanked them for their contributions. The taller one reached for her hand and had the audacity to kiss it as her rosy cheeks turned crimson. She bid them good day, and they reluctantly left the store. Her eyes roved over her treasures with both delight and astonishment until she glanced his way. She let out a soft gasp.

"Mr. Kerrington! I didn't see you there." She glanced at the clock and touched her hair self-consciously. "Can you flip the sign to *closed*? I von't be a moment!"

She disappeared as he did so and emerged a short while later with her hair tidied and her dress changed. This time, she'd let her hair down, as was slowly becoming fashionable, and it flowed over her shoulder in soft reddish-gold waves. It was tied with a green ribbon which also wrapped around her head. Her choice of dress was more subdued – a lilac affair with a straight skirt and minimal embellishment.

"You look charming," he said, feeling rather old and out-of-place. She seemed distracted as they made their way to The Tea Biscuit, answering him in single syllables. He wondered if she was thinking about the givers of all of those beautiful bouquets. "You must have many admirers. Perhaps you should open a flower shop."

She blushed deeply as she grinned at him. "I should, shouldn't I? Ever since you brought me flowers yesterday, all of my customers decided to as vell. It's so nice to have good friends, isn't it?"

Friends. The word stuck in his mind like the thorn of a rose. Is that all she saw him as, one of her friends?

"Those two young men seemed quite enamored of you," he ventured.

She waved his comment away, but her fanning hand said he'd struck a chord. "Oh my, I knew not vat to think. This has never happened before."

"What?"

"He proposed marriage to me!"

Lucas stopped dead in his tracks, causing her to spin around and almost run into him. Her face was now inches from his, and he forced himself *not* to put his arms around her. His deep voice quivered.

"What did you say?"

"I said I vould think about it," she replied after a pause. "I...I had no idea he liked me in that vay."

As her eyes found their way back to his, he thought he saw pain inside them. As if in confirmation, a tear escaped and tumbled down her cheek. He wiped it away with his handkerchief.

"I'm sorry," she whispered. "I'm not very *gut* company tonight."

Lucas threaded her arm back through his. "Perhaps dinner will cheer you up. I hear the molten fudge cake is delicious." She smiled at this, and he vowed that even if she wasn't in love with him, he would do his best to see her home happy.

Anne instantly regretted telling him about the proposal. It was a private matter between her and the fellow, and she shouldn't have revealed it. She already knew her answer, but she'd been so surprised that she'd given the poor man hope. But why did he propose? They'd known each other for years, and he'd never expressed an interest in her before.

Lucas was merry during dinner, but she could tell his heart wasn't in it. The relaxed camaraderie they'd had at the first seemed to have fizzled. Once at her front door, she wasn't ready for the night to end so gloomily. She invited him to partake of something hot to drink on her front porch swing. She settled next to him with her cup of tea, hoping he might put his arm around her.

Lucas sipped his coffee and thought about his ruined plans. A handsome, much younger man had proposed marriage to Anne. Would she be a fool not to accept him? He turned and found her watching him.

"May I ask you a question?" she said quietly.

"Of course."

"How did you get those scars?"

His hand instantly went to his face as his mind tumbled into the past. "In prison."

"Vas it as bad as they say?"

He wasn't sure what they said, but he answered truthfully. "It was horrible, but I deserved it."

She set down her tea cup and reached up to his face. Her soft fingers traced the lines before her hand cupped his cheek. "You didn't deserve this. No one vould." Her amber eyes glowed with the tenderness for which he longed, and he felt drawn to her.

"Anne," he slipped, reaching for her hand.

"*Ja*, Lucas?" Her fingers trembled in his grasp, and she tilted her face just enough for a kiss. He wanted to kiss her, to have everything said and done, but he held back.

"I should go. It's getting late." And the moment was broken. He stood slowly, his face turned away from her disappointment.

"Vill I see you soon?" she asked softly.

"Yes. I have much to do on the house, after all."

"May I come see it?"

He regarded her from across the dimly lit porch. "I'll think about it." She nodded her head, and he walked off into the night.

Anne thrilled at the invitation in her hand. Lucas had sent a note requesting her to bring a friend and meet him at his home after work. She'd immediately dispatched a request to Louisa Tiffany since she assumed Tilly wouldn't wish to go.

Earlier in the day, she had sent a reply to the other gentleman declining his proposal as gently as possible. Louisa appeared shortly before five with her baby boy Ian Peter, and the two friends set off to the Kerrington estate.

The façade of the stately home had been greatly improved. The glossy black front door and shutters, re-pointed bricks, and repaired porch had been even further enhanced by some formal landscaping and pots upon pots of brightly-colored chrysanthemums. Lucas opened the door and ushered them into a clean but sparse front hall.

"Pardon my mess, ladies. I haven't begun on the interior work except to do a thorough cleaning and sorting."

As Anne gazed about her, she noted with delight the cut-crystal chandelier, the deep mahogany paneling, and the old growth oak floors. "It's beautiful!"

Louisa, slightly less impressed, agreed with her. Anne reminded herself of her friend's own fine home and thought she preferred Lucas' instead. He led them through all of the rooms on the ground floor which, along with a good-sized parlor and elegant dining room, included a large kitchen, a well-stocked library, and a brightly-lit sewing room. His plans for the house made her eyes dance with glee, and she wondered what it might be like to be mistress of such a home. It was in one of these daydreams that Louisa excused herself to change little Ian Peter. She left Anne and Lucas alone in the spartanly furnished parlor.

"What do you think?" Lucas asked, coming over to her.

"I love it!" she exclaimed. "It's nothing like my own home."

"You have a lovely home."

"I do," she agreed, "but it vill never compare to this."

"Have you...have you answered that young man yet?" he asked, his hands fidgety. "I admit I can't stop thinking about it."

Her face grew hot, and she shook her head. "I refused him. I didn't love him enough to marry him."

Lucas smiled hesitantly in response. "I suppose that makes sense. Perhaps another suitor will catch your eye?"

One already has, she thought. *The problem is, he von't speak up!* She lost herself in his clear blue eyes until Ian Peter's fussy cries diverted her attention.

"Anne? Anne?" Louisa called, hurrying into the room. "I'm very sorry, but I really should take him home. Are you ready to go?"

"In a moment," Anne replied, wishing she never had to leave. She turned back to Lucas and made her apologies. Louisa had already headed to the front door when Lucas grasped Anne's hand tightly.

"Do you really like it, Anne? Does it suit your taste?"

"I do, Lucas, very much! I hope you vill invite me again ven it is finished."

"I will," he replied, bringing her hand to his lips. "You can count upon it."

Lucas congratulated himself. He'd been able to kiss her hand without incident. It was a small accomplishment, but he was proud of it all the same. Her skin had felt wondrously soft against his lips, but instead of impure thoughts, he found himself re-contemplating courtship. She had refused the other man. That meant her heart was still free. And she'd loved his home and the changes he was making. If he could only fill it with her presence as his wife, his life would be complete.

As he began diligent work on the inside of his home, he also laid the groundwork for the plans of his heart. His steady, heartfelt prayers and thorough Bible study had convinced him he should make a go for her hand. It was clear that she held him in special regard, but how special was yet to be seen.

His trips to the hardware store became more and more frequent, and he asked often for her opinion on his choices. If he could make his home a pleasant blend of them both, he would consider his job well done. The months flew by. He took her to dinner, to concerts and plays, and anywhere there was a crowd. He still didn't fully trust himself alone with her as her beauty grew day by day. Her smile upon seeing him made him hum for hours with love and delight. However, he still hadn't shared his hopes. That he would do tonight.

Anne dressed with extra care this evening, feeling that something special was afoot. She arranged her strawberry-blonde hair in soft curls, leaving a few loose about her ears. Her new crimson gown with its gathered waist and modestly puffed sleeves set her heart all aflutter. She looked like a woman in love, as of course, she was.

Lucas picked her up in his shiny black open-top carriage at a quarter after six. His blue eyes sparkled with appreciation, and he kissed her on the cheek for the first time.

"You look perfect, my dear," he whispered. She shivered happily from head to toe as he handed her into the carriage and set off at a brisk pace.

"Vhere are ve headed this evening? A restaurant? The opera?"

"No. I have something special planned. You'll see."

They trotted through town and turned into a familiar drive. She'd not been to his house unescorted since the first time she'd been there. Her stomach gave a nervous flutter as she remembered what Tilly had told her. Although her friend had resigned herself to the match, she still hadn't ceased to warn Anne to watch her back. Had she been wrong in putting her trust in this man?

As they rounded the bend, she gaped at the pleasing sight before her. Kerrington House was lit up, every window shining brightly in the dark evening. He pulled up to the front door, jumped out, and offered her his hand. As she stepped down, he put his arm around her waist.

"What do you think, Anne?"

"It's *wunderbar*! Does this mean you've finished?"

"Yes. Would you like to see inside?"

Her grin faltered. "Alone?"

"You won't be alone, darling," he replied, clasping her hand gently. "You can trust me."

She nodded, wondering if she was about to do something very foolish. He led her to the front door which he opened with a flourish. Her eyes darted from detail to detail as she breathed in the sight before her. Every surface gleamed with polish and luster. Rich colors and fabrics reminded her not only of Lucas, but also of how she had helped him make his choices. He placed his hand on the small of her back and whispered into her ear.

"Are you ready?"

"I...I think so," she replied with only a faint tremor.

He rolled open the pocket doors to the parlor and the sight took her breath away. Not only was it decorated with such love and care, it was filled with the faces of her dear friends. Tilly and Thomas, Louisa and Ian, Dr. and Mrs. Byrne, the Stevenses and Baileys, and right in the middle in front of the roaring fire stood her *mutter* and *vater* and her *bruder* Rolfe. She ran to kiss them, laughing and crying with overflowing joy. Everyone laughed and clapped along with her, and then all grew silent as she turned back to Lucas.

"Vhy did you do all this?" she asked, drawing closer to him. He grinned mischievously.

"I needed you to know you could trust me."

"I do, Lucas. I do trust you."

"Do you trust me enough to marry me?" She covered her mouth with her hand as he lowered himself to one knee and gently caressed her other hand. "Anne Freiburg, I love you with all of my heart and soul. Will you marry me and fill this house with love and laughter, knowing that I will be only yours from this moment forth?"

"Tonight?" she exclaimed.

He was puzzled for only a moment before he gave her a shy smile. "If you wish."

"Oh yes, Lucas, I vill marry you! Tonight, tomorrow, or venever you vant. I love you!"

Lucas stole a glance at his beautiful bride as they stood before Mr. Stevens. A well-worn Bible lay in his hands as he read passages about love and fidelity and took their vows. When the time was right, he pulled his mother's diamond ring from his pocket and slipped it onto her finger. Her amber eyes smiled as much as her mouth, and his heart leaped a mile.

"I now pronounce you man and wife," the preacher declared, and then, he added a wink. "You may now kiss your bride."

Lucas wasted no time gathering her into his arms. All of the waiting and preparation had only raised his anticipation, but he'd not expected the overwhelming love which coursed through him as he held his Anne for the first time. Someone whistled as she wrapped her arms around his neck, and he pulled away only slightly.

"Shall we continue this later?"

"*Ja*," she replied, glowing brighter than the brightest candle. "I'm looking forward to it!"

"So am I."

As they parted to receive congratulations and well wishes from their loved ones, his heart soared higher than the clouds. His home had been restored to its full potential, and he had a breathtaking bride to fill it. God had given him a second chance at life and at love. Nothing was going to stop him from living his new life to the fullest.

Thank you for reading my short stories!

If you enjoyed
Tales of Harriford Grange, Volume 1...

Check out my website

Authorelizabethjsmith.com

for information on my upcoming works, including

Tales of Harriford Grange, Volume 2: Mysteries of Harriford Grange
and
additional volumes of
Tales of Harriford Grange

Read the latest news on my blog or drop me a line. I'd love to hear from you!

Made in the USA
Columbia, SC
28 August 2020